The Summer
I Saved the World...
in 65 Days

Michele Weber Hurwitz

The Summer I SAVED the WORLD... in 65 DAYS

SCHOLASTIC INC.

No part of this publication may be reproduced, stored in a retrieval system, or transmitted in any form or by any means, electronic, mechanical, photocopying, recording, or otherwise, without written permission of the publisher. For information regarding permission, write to Ember, an imprint of Random House Children's Books, a division of Penguin Random House LLC, 1745 Broadway, New York, NY 10019.

ISBN 978-1-338-03009-9

12 11 10 9 8 7 6 5 4 3 2 1   16 17 18 19 20 21

Printed in the U.S.A.   40

First Scholastic printing, May 2016

To good things,
small and remarkable.
They matter.

It starts with Mrs. Chung.

And flowers.

Marigolds.

My grandmother believed in what she called STs—Simple Truths. This was one of her favorites: Things happen when they're meant to happen, and the sooner people realize that, the more content they'll be. Most people, she said, don't understand, even when those things are right in front of them.

Today, the first day of summer vacation, while I'm on the hammock in my side yard, listening to music and trying to figure out why my phone is being weird, and tanning, and letting my freshly painted toenails dry, am I meant to see Mrs. Chung hobbling around on her crutches? Is this one of those things that is meant to happen?

Mrs. Chung has lived next door to us for as long as my family has been here—nine years—and way before that. There was a Mr. Chung, and two kids, but he died and the kids grew up and moved away. So Mrs. Chung lives by herself in that big house. With Christmas lights strung across her trees all year round. Never on, not even in December. Kind of sad, the wires just hanging off those trees, like there's no one to light them for anymore.

She's leaning on her crutches, looking at two plastic trays of flowers in her front yard. Her wrinkled face is like a drawing on a paper fan, folded in disappointment. She's mumbling to herself and shaking her head and pointing with one crutch to where she always plants her flowers in the spring, around the neatly trimmed evergreen bushes.

Two things I am not: a genius, and the kind of person who goes out of her way to help people. The first one, I can wish for, but it simply isn't going to happen, and the second one, well, I really admire those types. It's just that I don't usually step up. I think a lot of people are like that. They let someone else take care of things.

I don't have to be a genius to figure out that Mrs. Chung can't plant the flowers with her leg in a cast. I'm watching her, the hammock rocking slowly in the breeze, when I remember how Mr. Chung used to shovel the sidewalk when we had big snows, and how he went all the way from his driveway to ours, even though we should have shoveled our part. But somehow we never got around to it. Dad was working late, my brother was lazy, and Mom couldn't stand the cold. Me? I guess I kept thinking one of them would do it eventually; plus I had tons of homework. Or another excuse that seemed important at the time.

Mrs. Chung goes into her garage and half pushes, half drags a chair over to the flower trays. She sits, pats her forehead with a tissue, and then leans down and takes out one marigold. She holds it for a few minutes, cradled in her hands. Then she pulls herself up with the crutches, places the flower gently on the chair, and goes inside.

For some reason, I start thinking about what Mr. Pontello told us on our last day of eighth-grade US history, everyone sweaty and hyper and impatient, aching to peel their legs from their seats and leave that classroom forever.

He said, "It is very often the ordinary things that go unnoticed that end up making a difference. As you embark upon your high school careers, be unnoticed, but be remarkable."

I think I was the only one listening.

The little boy from next door, Thomas, runs out of his open garage and starts hopping. From his grass to mine, and then all the way to Mrs. Chung's driveway.

He turns toward me and shouts, "Nina! I learned how to hop!"

"Great!"

"You have to switch feet," he says, out of breath but smiling big. "So one foot doesn't get too tired."

I touch the edge of a toenail to see if it's dry as Thomas hops over to Mrs. Chung's flower trays. He stops, then looks over at me. "Why are the flowers in here?"

I shrug.

He stares at them. "But how will they grow if they're not in the ground?" He hops over to the chair and picks up the wilting marigold. "Poor flower."

Thomas puts the flower down and hops all the way back to his house. Pretty good for a five-year-old.

Two birds are on the love seat at the edge of my patio. I watch their jerky head movements, like they're talking to each other in their secret bird language. *Go ahead,* I think. *No one else sits on the love seat anymore.*

All-weather wicker with dark green cushions that Mom ordered from a catalog a few summers ago. She kept saying, "It's all-weather; it won't fade or tear or stain. It will last forever. *Forever.*" She copied the layout exactly as it had been on the page in the catalog, right down to the vase of huge droopy white flowers on the all-weather wicker-and-glass table.

The day the furniture was delivered, Mom made a pitcher of lemonade, because that was in the catalog picture too, and we sat on the patio together, Mom and Dad and me and Matt. Mom poured the lemonade into fancy glasses and put strawberries on the rims. Dad made a joking toast to the new furniture. Matt and I clinked our glasses and took big swallows. But the lemonade was so sour that we both started coughing. Matt went inside, got the box of sugar, and started pouring it into the pitcher, mixing it with a long wooden spoon. Dad said, "Take it easy, Matthew" just as the box fell into the pitcher and the whole thing tipped over. Matt and I stared at Mom. What was she going to do? Would she get mad? He'd ruined the catalog picture. But Dad started laughing and said, "Who'd like some sugar-ade?" and Matt drank a whole glass after I dared him.

The love seat has become almost creepy now, part of the garden, with a long strand of ivy wrapped around one of the armrests and a huge spiderweb underneath.

A dry leaf twirls from a tree and lands next to the birds, and they fly off. Empty cushions. How sad—a love seat that needs love.

The last time I sat on it was with Grandma. Just her and me, in the quiet of our yard, holding hands. Hers were white and frail, bumpy with blue veins, and I tried to memorize the way they looked. She'd been sick for a while. Her heart was failing, and I knew she didn't have much longer.

It has been almost a year since she died. I get hit with these moments, when I miss her so terribly—and can't even think about what has happened with my family—that I don't know what to do, how to make it not hurt so much. I've tried running around the block and turning my music up really loud, but that helps for only a short time.

Sometimes it feels like the dull ache in my chest is going to spill all over, seep into my cracks and corners, and stay forever.

The warm breeze lifts my hair, skims the back of my neck, moves across the grass like an electric current.

And there it all is, right in front of me. My prompt, I guess you could say. Grandma's Simple Truth and the empty love seat and Mrs. Chung's empty garden. Thomas's question. Mr. Pontello's advice. Even Mr. Chung doing our shoveling all those winters.

Get up. Do something. Now.

I walk to Mrs. Chung's and peek through her window. She's stretched out on the sofa, exhausted, that big, thick white cast covering her leg. How'd she break it? I don't even know.

I find a little digging tool in our garage, then drag the first tray of flowers to Mrs. Chung's evergreen bushes. Every spring, she arranges her marigolds in curving waves of color—deep reds on the outside, a middle wave of oranges, to golden, then the lightest yellow. Like a sunset.

As I dig the first hole, I feel a little panicky that she'll come out and be mad or something. You know how adults can jump to the conclusion that teenagers must be doing something wrong.

I don't know what I'll say if she does come out, so I take the flower from the chair and just focus on patting it into the dirt. Then another, and another. And suddenly I have a row.

I get up and look in the window again. Mrs. Chung has fallen asleep, so I keep going.

No one is around. Mom and Dad—at work. Matt—BMIA. Brother Missing in Action. Friends—complicated.

It's just me and the flowers.

One hour later, I have strips of black dirt under my fingernails and crisscross impressions of grass on my knees, and my back and neck are really stiff. But when I soak the flowers with water from our hose, there is Mrs. Chung's sparkling, dripping marigold sunset, just the way it's supposed to be.

For the first time in my life, I didn't wait for someone else to step up.

And that is the beginning of everything.

I can't tell Jorie. She won't get it.

We both know we became friends because we're neighbors. She lives on the other side of Mrs. Chung. But when you look at us—her with the newest, smartest phone in one back pocket of her skintight jeans and a lip gloss and mascara in the other, and me in need of some reworking—I wonder how it has lasted this long. In first grade, when Jorie moved into the cul-de-sac, we had playdates and did the things first-grade girls do. That was enough back then.

But now? Jorie and I are in between two places.

Like an intermission between the first and second acts of a play. I'm not sure how things are going to end up.

It's Saturday afternoon and I'm in her room. As usual, she's doing twenty things at the same time: zooming back and forth between five open windows on her laptop, dissecting the advice in three beauty magazines, tapping on her phone, finding some music, talking nonstop. I'll say this: she's always been fun to watch.

I'm on her bed, trying to find the right-size mushy pillow to mold under my sore neck. There are about a dozen neon-colored ones to choose from.

Jorie pops her gum and blows a bubble, turns a magazine page. "Hey, did you see Mrs. Chung this morning?"

I sit up. "No. What about her?"

"She was walking around the sidewalk on her crutches, like, crying and all upset. Freaked out, talking to herself." Jorie looks at me. "Wait. I never remember, is she Chinese or Korean?"

"Korean."

"Oh, yeah. Anyway, so my dad went over to talk to her, and get this. Someone sneaked into her yard and planted her flowers."

"Really? Was she . . . mad? I mean, what did your dad say?"

"He said she was totally confused but also, like,

10

elated. Over flowers. That's kind of weird, don't you think? I mean, who would go plant someone else's flowers?"

"She was happy?" A funny feeling spreads through my chest, as if a rush of lighter air is shooting into my lungs.

Jorie tilts her head and half smiles. "Yeah."

I get up and look out Jorie's bedroom window. I have a perfect view of the marigolds, standing straight, reaching toward the sun. And Mrs. Chung was elated, Jorie said. What a great word. "Elated." The opposite of "deflated." How she was before.

"Nina!" Jorie is waving her arms.

"What?"

"Hello? I've been talking to you for the last two minutes. Have you heard anything I've said?"

I grin at her. "Yes, everything." And I did, in the background.

She sighs. "Sometimes I just get the feeling you're not all there."

"I'm here. Of course I'm here."

Jorie pulls a long string of gum from her mouth and winds it around her finger. "I was *saying* that my mom can drive us on the first day of summer school. I am not walking in by myself, like a loser."

"Okay."

I walk to her shelf and spot the picture frame from

her seventh birthday party, decorated with fake jewels, glitter, and foam stars. "You still have this?"

She laughs. "Apparently. I don't know why, though. I was such a dork."

"No, you weren't."

She gets up, takes the frame. "Yes, I was. Look, I couldn't even glue." She points to the dried spots where nothing is glued, then puts the frame back on the shelf, facedown. "Anyway, you know that was a sad birthday for me; we don't need to go there."

"In a way, Jor, it was a great birthday. If you think about it."

She shakes her head. "Uh-uh. Don't do your quality-over-quantity thing."

Jorie had invited the whole class, but just two other girls came besides me. Jorie hadn't known there was going to be another party at the same time. One of the cool girls. So you know how that goes. But the four of us decorated the frames and ate pizza and cake and tie-dyed T-shirts purple and green. I had a great time, but Jorie cried at the end, after the other two girls left. Told her mom to throw away the T-shirt and the rest of the cake. Said she was done with birthdays forever.

Jorie is studying a magazine page. "What about this top and shorts for the first day of summer school?"

I nod. "Cute."

"Do you like the crop top?"

"Yeah. That'll look good on you."

She had twenty-five friends at her thirteenth birthday party this year, so (a) she obviously wasn't done with birthdays, and (b) the cool girl who ruined her seventh birthday party was there, and Jorie insisted on sitting next to her at the restaurant.

Jorie stands and reaches for my hands, then examines my fingernails. "What's going on here?" She laughs. "Sit down. Your toenails are fine, but you are in serious need of a manicure."

In five seconds, she has emptied her bag of nail supplies onto the shaggy purple carpet. She picks up my right hand and starts filing. "You really shouldn't let your nails get this bad. I mean, it's important, you know?"

I jump as she nicks a piece of skin.

"Sorry."

"No problem," I say, squirming. "Anything for beauty, right?"

"Absolutely. Sit still." Jorie concentrates intently on the base coat, then two coats of light pink, blowing softly on each nail.

I look at her array of polish colors. "How come you always do pink for me?"

"Because your nails are so short. Can't go too dark. Besides"—she holds out her hands, with beautiful oval nails—"I'm red. You're pink. That's us."

She piles everything back into her bag. "You have to let them dry a good half hour."

"I know." I stand and go back to the window as she keeps talking. Her voice is a constant hum, like the air-conditioning that's on in my house from April to October, and the heat that's on from November to March. I have long suspected that the windows in my house don't really open and they're fake, just made to look like real windows. My parents have a serious issue with climate control. Control in general, really. Which might be one reason that my brother keeps his headphones on and his bedroom door closed whenever he decides to be home.

It's right then, when I'm standing in Jorie's room, that the idea starts to come to me. I look out onto the cul-de-sac, built in a crescent shape, one road in and out. Seven houses, eight including Jorie's, all basically the same style but different colors. Brown, white, tan, repeat. Even though this is northern Illinois, it makes me think of the Fertile Crescent we learned about in social studies. The cradle of civilization. A place where people settled down, lived in a community. Had neighbors.

And I see things from her window that are there every day but I never really notice. Toys scattered all over the Cantalonis' lawn because their three boys are full of energy and Mrs. Cantaloni is pregnant. Mr.

Dembrowski's neat house, the cleanest one by far, but he never comes out. Does he still live there? Is he even alive? What if he's dead in there and no one knows? And Eli Bennett's house at one end, with his little brother, Thomas, running around their driveway in a bathing suit and black cape, slicing a plastic sword through the air, fending off imaginary enemies.

Or maybe a more real kind of enemy that he senses is lurking around our quiet little neighborhood—connected houses but unconnected people.

Thomas darts behind a tree, then leaps out with his sword pointed forward. What does he see? He staggers backward, clutches his stomach, and falls to the ground.

Maybe it's not what he sees but what he feels. I feel it too. Something dark. We aren't the only ones with fake windows.

And I think again about Mrs. Chung's marigolds, and Mr. Pontello telling us to be remarkable but unnoticed, and Grandma saying things happen only when they're meant to happen.

But what if—really, *what if*—a person could play a part in that? Affect what's meant to happen?

Or maybe even alter it. In a good way.

3

I'm suddenly possessed with this crazy idea.

"Jorie, I have to go." I don't think she hears me. She's still talking, even as I walk down the stairs and open her front door.

"Wait!" she calls then. She's at the top of the stairs, pulling her hair into a bun. "Don't leave!"

"I need to do something right now. I forgot. Hey, thanks for painting my nails."

"Hold on. You need quick-dry." She dashes into her room, then runs down the stairs with a small bottle.

She grabs my hands and sprays the nails. "It hasn't been a half hour."

I smile. "Of course. Thanks again."

She blows a huge bubble that pops on her nose.

I laugh while she makes a heart shape with her fingers, the gum still all over her face. I heart her back.

Jorie hugs me. "You're the best."

"You too."

At home in my mismatched room, a relief after the brightness of Jorie's, I flip through my eighth-grade assignment notebook and count the days of summer. Sixty-five before the first day of high school.

The only thing I'm doing is a summer school class (Art Form I) and reading the two books for freshman accelerated English. Jorie's around, but my friends from school, the group I was kind of sort of in last year, went on an adventure trip to the Pacific Northwest. I guess I could have gone too, but I'm not really a rugged, mountain-climbing, risk-taking person. Okay, the truth is, they never officially asked me to go. And . . . I don't think I was ever really *in* their group. We hung out mostly because we were all on the basketball team.

So. Here I am. Back to the idea. What if, for these sixty-five days, I do one good thing every single day that is meant to happen? By my meaning it to happen.

Sixty-five good things.

I'll have to have some ground rules.

Because everything in this world does.

They will have to be small, unnoticed things, but remarkable and amazing in their smallness and unnoticed-ness. Like planting the marigolds. They can't cost anything, because I have seven dollars in my wallet. And mostly they'll need to be anonymous.

No one can know it's me.

Nina Ross. Thirteen. Five foot one. Contacts or glasses, depending on the day. Medium-length straightish brown hair, and eyes that Matt used to call Nina green-a. Two beauty marks on my cheek, but I'm not really beautiful. Interesting-looking at best. Which is all right; I'll take interesting.

Speaking of. I hear a noise from my brother's room and walk across the hall. His door is open a sliver, so I peer through the crack. Headphones on. Drumming his fingers on his desk. Eyes closed.

"Matt?"

He doesn't hear my voice. Or if he does, he chooses to ignore me.

I stand there for a second, hoping he'll open his eyes; then I go back to my room.

In my closet, I find the poster board with my science project on the Florida Everglades and flip it over. I draw a wide, curving crescent, then a square for each of the houses in our cul-de-sac. If you're standing in the street facing the houses, on the left end is Eli Bennett's, then my house, then Mrs. Chung's, then Jorie's. Next to Jorie is Mr. Dembrowski, then the Cantalonis, then the Millmans. The last house is empty, with a For Sale sign. The Dixons were foreclosed on last year after Mr. Dixon lost his job. The house is looking kind of creepy, with overgrown grass and weeds, bald dandelion stems, even a couple of loose shutters.

I turn the blank pages of my assignment notebook, then trace my finger around on the poster board. The way I've drawn it, the houses look like they're separate little squares floating in space.

Everything good I've ever done before has been because someone told me to do it. "Don't forget to bring in money for the holiday gift drive." "Donate your unused school supplies—just drop them in the box by the office." "Buy a T-shirt for charity." "Add to the Thanksgiving food basket for a needy family." Quick, easy.

Our front door slams. From my fake window, I see Matt get into his old Jeep and drive away.

There's a blotchy dark spot on the street where it was parked. Dad will be mad. He'll say, *It must be leaking oil.* Mom might look up from her laptop, tell Matt to get it fixed. *Wasn't the deal that you'd be more responsible, Matthew?* They'll focus on the *car,* how something must be wrong with the *car*. Matt will stand there, silent, his face tight, and I'll be on the stairs, listening.

If Grandma was here, she'd look at the oil stain and wink at me. Come up with an ST about what we leave behind. How nothing is accidental. I'd get it in a second, then share a random thought with her, and she'd get that. In a second.

I don't say my random thoughts out loud anymore, because there's no one to get them. I've tried with Jorie, but she gives me strange looks. I didn't even try with the basketball group. People would think they're weird. *I'm* weird. What if I go through high school and, um, you know, *life,* without someone who gets me? Knows me?

I think about the love seat and wonder if there are any talking birds sitting on it today. Then I get that urgent sense again. *Do something.*

So much is not good.

I prop the poster board against a wall and close my assignment notebook.

Sixty-five things. I've already done the first one. What's another sixty-four?

I can't wait to get started.

Days two, three, and four, I clean up all the toys in the Cantalonis' yard, organizing them neatly by the side of their garage; put a Hershey's Kiss in the Millmans' mailbox; and snip a rose from my mother's garden (which she never looks at, so she won't know it's missing), tie a ribbon around it, and leave it on Mr. Dembrowski's doorstep.

On day five, I place a penny (heads up) in each of my neighbors' mailboxes to bring them good luck. And one in mine (so no one will suspect).

On day six, Mrs. Millman calls the police.

Which is not unusual. She called the police last month because she was convinced a repairman was hiding in the ducts in her attic. Before that she called them when she thought her miniature poodle, Beanie, had radon poisoning.

There's a police car parked in front of her house. "*Someone* has been sneaking around and *doing* things," she says loudly to the officer, her arms crossed tightly. They're standing on the sidewalk, and I'm sitting in our hammock under the maple tree, my heart beating very fast.

"What kinds of things?" He pulls out a small notebook.

She stamps her foot. "Trespassing!"

I hadn't thought of it that way. I mean, I live here too.

"Anything missing from your home?" the officer asks.

"Not that I'm aware of."

"Any locks tampered with? Forced entry?"

"No."

"What, exactly, was trespassed, Mrs. Millman?"

"There was a Hershey's Kiss in my mailbox three days ago," she says. "I didn't eat it. I have it in case you want to test for fingerprints, or poison. And yesterday, there was a penny!"

The officer lowers his sunglasses and raises his eyebrows. "You called the police because a Hershey's Kiss and a penny were in your mailbox?"

"Yes, and *someone* moved all the toys in the Cantalonis' yard. Mrs. Cantaloni asked her boys, and they didn't do it. Plus there's the *situation* of Mrs. Chung's marigolds. Who planted them? It's a mystery."

The officer taps his pen on the notebook. Thomas Bennett chooses this moment to rush out of his house in his underwear, his cape flying behind him. He runs around the sidewalk and pokes the plastic sword into Mrs. Millman's calf.

"Whoa." The officer pulls him away. "Take it easy, there, Batman."

"I'm not Batman! Batman doesn't have a sword!" Thomas shouts.

"Thomas!"

That would be Eli.

Thomas takes off toward the empty Dixon house. He runs through the weeds that used to be their front lawn, and around the back. Eli dashes after him, and a minute later, Eli is carrying Thomas on his shoulders, with Thomas whipping the sword through the air. Eli's hands are securely around Thomas's ankles, and he's walking kind of springy, so Thomas is bouncing a little with each step. And giggling. Thomas's hair is long, over his ears and almost into his eyes. Eli puts him down on their driveway.

"Mrs. Millman," the police officer is saying, "there's no crime that I can detect. I'll check around your house, but it doesn't sound like there's anything here for me to put into a report."

Mrs. Millman straightens her flowered skirt. "*Something* is going on. You'll see. And when I call you the next time, believe me, it'll be more than Hershey's Kisses!"

"Okay." The officer closes his notebook. "I'll just take a look around."

He goes toward the back of the Millmans' house, then walks through the Cantalonis' backyard, and Mr. Dembrowski's. The rose is still on his front step. Looking very wilted.

"Lemonhead?"

I look up to see Eli standing next to the hammock, holding out a box.

My throat is suddenly very dry, and I reach out my hand. He pours two into my palm.

"Crazy, huh?" Eli says.

"Yeah," I breathe.

"How are ya, Neen?"

This is what I want to say: *When did you get so tall, and do you remember writing your name twenty-three times in chalk on my driveway with a backward E when we were six?*

But I say, "I'm fine."

He sits on the grass, and we both watch Mrs. Millman pacing in front of her house, talking excitedly on her phone.

"I think if I was Mr. Millman, I'd take a lot of business trips," Eli jokes.

I smile.

Thomas leaps out from the bushes in between my house and the Bennetts'. "I'm beating the bad guys!" he yells, thrashing his sword. "The crinimals!"

"Criminals," Eli corrects him, but Thomas is off again. Eli stands. "I hope he grows out of this underwear-and-cape stage by the time he goes to school. Or else he won't make a lot of friends."

"Or maybe he will," I say, laughing. "I'd want to be friends with a superhero."

Eli shakes his head. "You know what I mean."

He goes after Thomas. The officer gets into his car and sits there for a while with the motor running, then drives away. Mrs. Millman stomps back into her house as Mrs. Cantaloni speeds off in her minivan with her boys in their baseball gear, buckled in. I haven't seen Mrs. Chung since I planted her marigolds. Everyone's windows are shut, front doors are closed, garage doors are down. My parents had dinner with a client and got home so late last night, I didn't even see them.

I feel something, someone, near me, behind the hammock, and I whip my head around. Thomas is

25

slithering on the ground, propelling himself with his elbows.

"The policeman didn't get the crinimals," he pants. "It's up to me!" He jumps up and leans close to my face. I smell his little-boy sweat—sweet, like fresh-cut grass. His nose grazes my cheek as he whispers, "And guess what? I have a magic coin!"

He opens his fist to show me a penny.

5

On her way to work, Jorie's mom drops us at entrance fourteen of the high school's west building, which is connected to the east building by an environmentally friendly atrium. The school is bigger than some colleges. I am terrified to actually go here.

Jorie talked nonstop during the ride, asking if I could see the pimple on her chin under the cover-up and saying first days are *so* hard and she's *so* glad she has me, but then, we're not inside two seconds when she spots this girl in her summer school class—the blow-off Intro to Computers One—and runs to catch up with her. The girl has one of those names that's also a place. Savannah or Dakota or Antarctica. She and Jorie are both wearing crop tops.

I'm in art with the rebellious, darkish people. A couple of guys in combat boots and black jeans with little chains hanging from the belt loops. A girl in a black T-shirt with skulls on it. A lot of black clothes here. Scary.

When we were still in junior high and went to the orientation for high school, they kept advising us to take a summer school class so we'd get used to life here and meet kids from the other junior highs. I chose art because I like to draw, even though my drawings never turn out as I imagine they're going to.

As I head toward the back of the room, a heavy girl with ripped black-and-white-striped tights and blue jean shorts turns around and stares at me with the kind of look that says *Who are you, and what are you doing here?* Then this spike-haired guy next to her does it too. Like her stare is contagious.

Oookay. Maybe I didn't think this through. This does not feel like the place where I'll meet new people. I take a seat in the last row, feeling like I glow in the dark with my normal white T-shirt. I see two girls I recognize from junior high, but they're sitting close, talking. There's one quiet girl (not wearing black), but she doesn't look my way.

For the first half hour, we talk about what we're going to do for the next eight weeks. Then we start our color wheels. My primaries turn out fine, but I have a serious mixing issue when it comes to the secondary colors. The teacher, Ms. Quinlan, who looks like she used to be rebellious and darkish when she was in high school, stops at my desk. She has ten piercings on her ears, plus stubby chewed fingernails.

"Make sure you take equal amounts of the colors when you mix," she comments.

I nod, and she moves on, pauses at the heavy girl's desk. "Nice," she says, looking at her color wheel, then holds it up to show everyone else.

The only word I say all morning is "Here" during attendance. Great first day.

Jorie and I have to take the bus home, which she isn't happy about. The air is hot and thick, even with all the windows open, and her cheeks are bright pink. Like her tank top.

We see Eli getting into a car with some boys. Jorie cranes her neck and watches the car drive away. "Isn't that Eli's friend Tyler? And his older brother? I think he's a junior. He must have his license."

I'm looking at the syllabus for art. Drawing, painting, ceramics. Wow.

"What class is Eli taking?"

I shrug. "I don't know."

Jorie leans back in the seat and exhales dramatically. "I'm going to tell you a secret." She says this all the time, so nothing with her is ever really secret.

"What?"

"This is the summer Eli and I are going to get together. I've got it all planned. I'm going to get him to ask me to homecoming. We'll start our freshman year as a couple. The boy next door. How cute is that?"

Technically he's the boy next door to me.

You know that memory with the chalk? Eli writing on my driveway? Yeah, well, Jorie was there too, decorating his backward *E*s with flowers and peace signs. Even at six, she had a little thing for him.

"He's gotten so cute, hasn't he?" Jorie breathes.

"Yeah, I guess. You like him?"

"Duh."

"Oh. Really? Eli?"

"Yes," she sighs. "Why do you sound surprised? It's there. I feel it. Certain things, you just *know*."

The bus pulls up at the entrance to our cul-de-sac, and the driver opens the doors.

"Well, good luck with that," I say as Jorie tears off toward her house.

"Text me later!" she calls, running, her tote bag banging against her hip.

"My phone's still being weird!" I shout.

"Get a new one already! Your phone is ancient!

From, like, when? Sixth grade?" She slams her front door.

I dropped my phone, and now it randomly decides when it wants to work right. I dropped my last phone too. The thing is, Dad said if I broke this one, I had to pay for another. With what, I don't know.

No one's around, except Thomas, who salutes me from his driveway. He's throwing his sword into the air and catching it. It falls more times than it ends up in his hands.

"I'm practicing for the bad guys," he yells. "You gotta do these tricks!"

I smile and give him a thumbs-up.

I look around at the houses. I'm on good thing number six, but after the police episode with Mrs. Millman, I missed a day. Should I keep this up? What if she finds out and gets me in trouble somehow? That wasn't part of my plan.

"They're all around here! Hiding and stuff!" Thomas says. "You see them?"

I laugh. "Yeah!"

I pause in my driveway. Mrs. Chung's marigolds are wilting. She can't possibly water them. I look toward Mrs. Millman's. No sign of her. I get that air-rushing-into-my-lungs feeling again as I quickly turn on our hose and start spraying the flowers before I change my mind. While I'm watering, the mail truck drives by. I get Mrs. Chung's pile from her mailbox and leave it at her front door.

Number six. And seven.

"Pow!" Thomas roars, making a tough face. "I got one! I got a bad guy, Nina!"

I wave at him. He leaps high, then does a somersault on the grass.

Hmm. . . . Good thing done. Bad guy gone.

Mrs. Millman or no Mrs. Millman, I don't want to stop.

It feels right to keep going. I sound like Jorie talking about Eli, but that's totally different. I don't get exactly why I know; I just *do*.

6

This is how dinners are at my house these days.

I'm starving by six p.m., but Mom and Dad are still at work. So I make myself something like macaroni and cheese or a frozen pizza, then debate between a healthy dessert (apple) or an unhealthy one (Reese's). Most times, I end up eating the Reese's in two bites. (With milk to take the edge off the guilt.)

Matt goes to Subway with his friends. How do I know? The floor of his car is littered with paper napkins, and his T-shirt has that bread smell.

My parents usually get home around seven-thirty

with square black plastic carryout containers. They are divorce lawyers, in their own practice. Fine and Ross, Attorneys-at-Law. My mother is Fine. (She kept her maiden name, and she is not really fine much of the time.) My dad is Ross (his last name, mine too). They're on a mission to get to the top. Of something. They take one of the earliest trains into the city every day and the six-thirty train back. Sometimes an even later one. From what I can tell, their job is to get the person who is divorcing the other person the most money possible. The Fine and Ross formula: divorce + money = happiness.

Mom texts me every morning: *All okay?* and Dad calls in the afternoon when I'm home from summer school, but I hear him shuffling papers in the background. Matt's supposed to be checking in on me. But he's at work a lot, and then, just, out.

Summers when I was younger, someone was always home when I got off the day camp bus—Matt or Mom or Grandma. And after camp ended, Grandma took me on special outings: afternoon tea at a fancy downtown hotel; and to the butterfly house, where if you stood still and quiet, one might land on you.

When my parents finally get home, they spread out at the kitchen table with their containers of food, laptops, and phones, and they work and eat and strategize. For months, they've been immersed in the biggest case of their careers, apparently the kind they've always wanted. Dad told me, "Divorces don't come any more high profile than this," and Mom, while she was dipping a lettuce leaf in fat-free dressing and reading an email, said, "This case has catapulted us to an entirely new category." Like they were holding on to those wobbly high-jump poles and hurtling over the Lawyer Wall of Fame.

The other night, she took a minute to ask if everything was going all right in my life.

I said, "Sure."

She nodded. "We'll talk more later, okay? I just need to finish something." Her phone rang, and Dad said, "It's Melanie." (The big, important client.) Mom answered immediately.

If I said my family was different once upon a time, no one would believe me.

But I swear it was.

I remember me and Matt and Mom and Dad before we got separated. Or divorced, I guess you could say, but still living in the same house.

Everything's faded, like the few photos I have of my grandma. I don't like to look at those, because I get too sad.

But if I do allow myself to think about the memories, it's like watching a video of how family dinners used to be. There's one from when I was around nine . . . before Grandma lived with us . . . when Mom and Dad had low-profile clients . . . and before the whole thing that happened with Matt.

The video is funny, and sweet: Dad cutting spaghetti with a knife and fork because it was easier to eat, Matt sticking his foot on my chair and me telling him to stop (but laughing because his toes were tickling my leg), and Mom smiling at us while she sliced a loaf of garlic bread, crumbs scattering across the table like pebbles.

Was that really us?

Sometimes that video feels like it's someone else's. A different, happier family.

7

Mrs. Millman has pulled a patio chair around to her driveway. Every morning when Jorie and I leave for summer school, she's sitting out there with a newspaper, holding it the way people do in old detective movies, when they're pretending to read but are really snooping on someone. I heard her tell Mrs. Cantaloni that she's watching so she can find out who is *doing things*.

Should I tell her it's an inside job?

I think I've figured out a good strategy, though. When I get home, Mrs. Millman's guard chair is folded up and she's walking around with Beanie on a tight leash. After Beanie takes care of business, Mrs. Millman, being a considerate, law-abiding neighbor, picks up the poop in a little blue bag, deposits it in her garbage can, and brings Beanie inside. She comes back out with a tote bag over her shoulder that says MAH-JONG, ANYONE?, then gets into her car and drives off. Some of Grandma's friends played that game, with the tiles that have Chinese symbols.

Mrs. Millman has a very predictable schedule. With her two-hour mahjong outings every weekday afternoon, that's more than enough time to go ahead with my plan.

Not only do I worry about Mrs. Chung (number eight: untangled a plastic bag caught on one of her trees; and number nine: hung up the wind chimes that had fallen off the hook by her door), but I've been concerned about Mr. Dembrowski. Does he have food in there? How old is he now? Maybe he's become a hoarder and can't get out the door. Is that why no one ever sees him?

Mr. Dembrowski used to be the guy all us little kids were scared of. There's one in every neighborhood. He yelled when a ball went into his yard, or someone ran across his grass, or someone left their bike on his sidewalk.

When Jorie, Eli, and I were eight, we were playing

hide-and-seek on a sweltering summer night. Our cheeks were red and hot and we were buzzing with the electricity and heart-pumping thrill that happens when a neighborhood goes from day to night and you're finally old enough to stay up and be outside in the dark.

Eli and I were hiding from Jorie. We were in back of Mrs. Chung's house, behind a row of bushes, hugging our knees tight. I could hear the sweet piano music coming from her house and wondered if she was giving a lesson. Jorie's voice was getting madder. "Where are you guys? This isn't funny!" But Eli put a finger up to his lips and shook his head. He took my sweaty hand. I swear I could feel his heartbeat through his fingers.

After Jorie found us, someone—and to this day, I don't know who—ran through Mr. Dembrowski's flower bed. He had all these unusual kinds, fragile and exotic, but how were we supposed to know that? We were just trying to find the best hiding places.

It had just rained, and in the morning, there were shoe prints and trampled flowers. Mr. Dembrowski marched over to each of our houses and demanded a shoe. So he could match the print.

This was one of the times when my mother was not fine. She flipped on her lawyer switch and made a federal case about not turning over my shoe. It could have been anyone, she said. Jorie's dad got mad too (he is a very high-strung stock trader) and said Mr. Dembrowski was making too much out of it and we were just kids. Eli's parents were getting divorced about that time, so no one was even there when Mr. Dembrowski rang their bell.

That was when Eli started to pull away, and I get it, I really do. He had a lot going on. His parents got back together just long enough to have Thomas; then they split again. Messed-up normal.

I've always felt guilty about Mr. Dembrowski's flower bed. We all should have taken the blame. But our parents argued us out of the situation.

So good thing number ten will be for Mr. Dembrowski.

I find a dusty package of brownie mix on the top shelf of our pantry. The expiration date is this month, but I figure that's okay. I'm pretty good at baking when I concentrate. I preheat the oven, follow the directions, and mix with exactly fifty strokes like the package says.

Then I start a sketch for art while the chocolate smell fills the kitchen. The assignment is to do a realistic drawing of a normal household item, with shading, light and dark, and good composition. I choose to draw a chair, which somehow ends up looking like a house on stilts.

I take the brownies out and stick in a toothpick. Done. Let them cool. Cut into neat squares, and place ten (for good thing number ten) on a paper plate, then slide it into a ziplock bag.

Mrs. Millman is at mahjong, and no one else is in sight, so it's easy to walk across to Mr. Dembrowski's house. I stand at his front step for a second. Whoa! The rose is gone.

Every shade is pulled down. I have no evidence that he actually took the rose. It could have blown away, or been carried off by an extremely strong ant population, or even been eaten by Beanie.

I leave the plate by his door.

When I come in, Matt is leaning against the kitchen counter, wearing dark sunglasses and a cap, eating a brownie.

"Matt," I say happily. "Welcome to the downstairs."

"Funny," he says, wiping the back of his hand across his mouth and taking another brownie. "Why'd you make these?"

"I just felt like it. How are they?"

He smiles at me with chocolate all over his teeth. "Good."

"So, are you in disguise?"

He lowers the glasses and raises an eyebrow. Doesn't answer.

I put the pan in the sink and run water into it. I just

know he's going to finish the brownie and disappear again. "Hey, um, are you doing anything? Wanna hang out? Maybe . . . play cards?"

He shrugs.

"Remember that time we played war for hours? We said we'd play till someone won."

Matt laughs. "No one ever wins war."

"You won that time."

"I did? Oh, yeah."

I cross my arms. "I want a rematch."

He pushes up his sunglasses. "Can't. Got some stuff to do. See ya."

He goes out. I look at the gross brownie water.

Nice chatting with you, Matt.

8

In the morning, the plate of brownies is still there. I can see it from my window. This makes me sad, and more worried about Mr. Dembrowski.

In our basement storage room, there's a treasure trove of stuff in boxes and bags: unopened gifts my parents received from clients, things they bought and never used, and other random items.

I have good uses for them.

11. I wrap up a package of gel foot pads, the kind for shoes, and leave them for Eli's mom, Mrs. Bennett, who is a nurse and stands for hours at a time.

12. I leave an aromatherapy candle for Jorie's dad because he needs to calm down.

13. There's a box of wrapped cigars that Dad has never even touched, and I have this feeling that Mr. Millman is the kind of man who would like to smoke a cigar once in a while. Living with Mrs. Millman can't be easy.

It's when I'm sneaking the cigars to the Millman house that I realize the plate of brownies is no longer on Mr. Dembrowski's front step.

I'm elated. I have a warm feeling inside, like a tiny flame was lit.

14. When Jorie drops her lip gloss on the bus, even though it's slightly rude that she has her back to me and is talking to the girl across the aisle, I catch it with my foot, pick it up, and slide it into her tote bag.

That night, I see a small red glow across the street and I can just make out Mr. Millman standing in his driveway, smoking a cigar. He looks content.

Then I hear voices. Jorie's. The bounce of a basketball. And . . . Eli's laugh.

I go downstairs and pass Mom and Dad, who are working at the kitchen table.

"Hey, hon," Mom says, not looking up but waving in my direction. "Did you eat?"

"Yeah. I had a frozen pizza."

"Nina," Dad says, "could you grab that bottle of seltzer from the fridge?"

I hand it to him, then poke my head out the front door.

Jorie and Eli are in his driveway. It looks like they're playing one-on-one, and Jorie is going for a gold medal in flirting. She's wearing the shortest butt-hugging shorts I've ever seen. With a tight, low-cut tank top. Dark purple, glittery. Plus she's doing this fake, high-pitched giggling. That's not how she laughs. "Show me how to do a layup," she says.

Eli puts his hand on top of hers and helps her dribble. Then when they get close to the basket, he picks her up so she can shoot the ball.

She sort of falls back into him as he lets her down. And fake giggles. And shakes out her long hair. The ball rolls onto the grass, and they're standing really close.

I feel sick. Like I'm watching something I shouldn't. She's serious about Eli and homecoming. Usually Jorie's ideas come and go in a flash.

Eli and Jorie don't see me, and I go back inside, a little shaky.

Mom's cleaning up their papers. She's been wearing her short hair gelled back behind her ears. Not even one strand came loose all day.

"I'm running to the grocery store," she says. "Do you want anything special?"

I hesitate. "You know what I really want?"

She piles the papers into her briefcase. "What?"

"Grandma's carrot ring."

She looks up, her face tight. "I can't make that. I don't even know where the recipe is."

A long second goes by. She picks up her purse, takes out her keys.

"We're out of frozen pizza," I say, and shrug.

"Okay. I'll get a few."

Yeah.

Grandma used to make her carrot ring a lot when we went to her apartment for dinner. It was one of the best things I've ever tasted, and I don't even like carrots that much.

Dad's on the sofa, feet up on the table, flipping through channels. As I pass him, he says, "What's the matter?"

I keep walking. "Nothing. I'm fine."

"Really?"

"Yes." Which is completely untrue.

I can still hear Jorie's and Eli's voices outside. Why am I upset? I mean, if they like each other . . . I just didn't think Eli was like that. Going for the butt-hugging shorts and obvious flirting.

But I'm thinking about the Eli from when we were

little. The quiet, protective boy who wouldn't let go of my hand that summer night we hid from Jorie. The funny, sweet, awkward Eli who gave me a crumpled Valentine with a picture of a cartoon truck with goofy-looking eyes that said *Sending you truckloads of* [scratched-out word] *on Valentine's Day. Your friend, Eli Bennett.* When I held it up to my lamp, I could tell the scratched-out word was "love."

Do I even know the Eli from now?

And then this hits me: Do I know Jorie anymore?

9

On the way to summer school, Jorie doesn't say anything about Eli, and I don't ask. I show her my chair drawing. "What do you think this is?"

She tilts her head. "I don't know . . . one of those old-fashioned tables where you do your hair and makeup?"

"You mean a vanity?"

"Yeah."

I sigh. "No. It's a chair."

She squints. "Oh, okay. I see it." Then she laughs. "I told you that you should've done the computer class with me. It's easy. And I'm meeting so many new people. *Lots* of cute guys."

Great.

In art, when I hold up my drawing, people guess a table, a bed, and a spaceship. But then the quiet girl, Sariah, says softly, "Is it a chair?" I almost want to hug her.

Ms. Quinlan gives me some tips about shading and dimension, and while I'm reworking the drawing, I glance at Sariah. She's tall and skinny, with smooth brown skin and braces. Long, straight dark hair. Her drawing is a bowl of fruit, and it's really good. When it's time for the break, I try to catch her eye, but she walks out ahead of me and sits near a group in the commons. I hang at the edge of Jorie's group.

By the end of class, my chair is starting to look more like a chair. Ms. Quinlan says, "Better. Keep going."

And I do.

I bring Mrs. Chung's mail to her door every day, but I'm not counting that anymore. It's just my routine; I'm pretty sure she thinks it's the mailman. I drop off two more plates of something sweet at Mr. Dembrowski's door (fifteen, sixteen). Either the squirrels or Mr. Dembrowski take them, because they're both gone the next day. I make chocolate chip cookies—just the break-and-bake kind—and leave some on Matt's desk (seventeen). The empty dish is in the sink the next morning.

When she's not at mahjong, Mrs. Millman has been stalking the cul-de-sac with Beanie. She told Mrs. Cantaloni that she's training Beanie as a watchdog. She said Beanie's grandfather was a killer. Excuse me for saying, but that scrappy little poodle does not look very much like a watchdog. Real intruders won't be scared off by Beanie Millman.

Funny, but the more upset Mrs. Millman becomes, the more it makes me want to keep doing the good things.

I thought it would be hard to think of them. But it's easy. I see something that needs my attention, and I do it. Random things present themselves every day. I keep counting, and Mrs. Millman keeps patrolling, like we're in a silent race, Nina Ross versus Myrna Millman. Anonymous good versus suspicion. Who will win? I don't know, but I really hope she doesn't freak out and call the police again.

I'm outside on Friday afternoon, *still* working on the chair drawing. It's due on Monday. I never want to draw another chair. The three Cantaloni boys are pitching and catching on their front lawn. I always mix up their names; they all start with *J.*

They're copies of each other—dark hair, stocky, in

the same blue striped T-shirt: one small, one medium, one large. The youngest kid looks close to Thomas's age, and I wonder why they don't play together.

The tallest one pitches the ball to the middle kid. He hits a pop fly, and the younger kid does his best to get under it, but as he's stepping back, he's getting closer and closer to the weeds that used to be the front lawn of the Dixon house. He stops as the ball lands in the field of weeds, and they all just stare. I suppose that house is to them what Mr. Dembrowski's was to me, Jorie, and Eli. The stuff of ghost stories and nightmares.

"You suck!" the older Cantaloni boy yells to the younger brother, who runs inside their house, crying.

"You get it!" the older one says to the middle guy.

"No, you!"

"I'll give you my best baseball card."

"Forget it. I'm not going in there."

"I'll let you use my mitt for the rest of the day."

"Uh-uh."

They look at the weeds, where something makes a rustling sound. The boys glance at each other, then tear into their house.

I put my sketchbook on the ground and go to the edge of the Dixons', trying to see the ball and what was making the sound.

I take two mini steps into the weeds; they're as high

as my knees in some spots, and scratchy against my bare legs. I hear the rustle again and see the weeds by the front window move. Must be a squirrel or a rabbit.

I haven't ever been this close to the Dixon house. The family was here for just three years. In that whole time, I found out only that there was a husband, wife, and a kid in college. They kept their shades down, never planted flowers, and closed their garage as soon as they pulled their cars in. Dad joked that they were in the Mafia. Mom thought they just kept to themselves.

I start walking slowly, parting the weeds, looking for the baseball and keeping my eye on the spot where the rustling occurred.

I'm in front of a regular house, in a quiet, boring suburb, the same as thousands of suburbs everywhere, but with the overgrown weeds, it doesn't seem like the Fertile Crescent but like the Florida Everglades. What if the rustling is from a snake, or an alligator, or a panther? Impossible, since our most terrifying wildlife around here is a coyote. Still, I get a little shaky.

Just when I spot the baseball, a flash of coppery red fur swishes through the weeds and runs into the middle of the street. I catch my breath, crouch, and freeze. Will it see me? Attack? Where is Beanie, the great watchdog?

The red fox turns and looks me straight in the eye as

I peek out from among the tips of the weeds. The fox is beautiful, wild, and captivating. Its ears are pointed up, and its tail is long and thick, lighter than the rest of its coat.

It takes off, running between Jorie's and Mrs. Chung's houses. Then it's gone.

As I slowly stand, my legs shaking, I see Mrs. Chung, leaning on her crutches. She hobbles to the end of her driveway.

I pick up the baseball and toss it onto the Cantalonis' lawn (eighteen) and head toward Mrs. Chung, who is wearing a sock and a sandal on the normal foot.

She picks up a crutch and points in the direction the fox ran. *"Kumiho,"* she whispers.

That doesn't sound good. "What?"

"Nine-tailed fox. Korean legend. Evil."

I stop. "Evil?"

She nods and looks at the sky. "Fox is often a bad sign."

I follow her gaze. The sky is clear and blue, not one cloud. Evil? *No,* I want to say. *Good. Good things.*

"Mrs. Chung—" I try to think of one of Grandma's STs, something reassuring, but Mrs. Chung hurries back inside as quickly as she can on crutches.

I glance around. Still. Silent. The lone baseball on the Cantalonis' lawn.

There's movement in Mrs. Chung's window. I see

her parting the drapes with her hand. Now I think of what to say: *The fox is gone. And it had only one tail. So it couldn't have been the* kumiho. *Really, no* kumiho *here.*

I pick up my sketchbook. It's eighty-five degrees out, but I get goose bumps on my arms as Mrs. Chung lets the drapes fall back.

Thank God the Cantaloni boys choose this moment to tumble out their front door and seize the baseball like a miracle has happened.

They don't even question it, just start their game.

"Catch it next time, you moron!" the older one yells.

"Shut up, Jack!"

I sink to the grass. Jack. The oldest boy's name is Jack.

I've never been terrific at finishing projects. This past year, I started a scrapbook, a journal, three books, daily yoga stretches, and a beauty routine involving a weekly mask and blackhead strips. I didn't continue any of them. I got bored, distracted. But the sixty-five things are something I *want* to finish. I *have* to. They're sneaky and fun and exciting—thinking of them, figuring out how to keep them secret. Every time, I get this filled-up, kind of powerful feeling. Strong. Hopeful. I wish I could tell Grandma. And my teacher, Mr. Pontello. They'd know what I mean.

19. Matt's been working a lot at his cashier job at the pool. His car's a mess, and I don't want Mom and Dad to get mad, so I clean it out while he's in the shower. What I find: fifteen Subway napkins; one black, stretchy headband; a white sock; seven pens; two pencils; gum wrappers; a torn ace of diamonds card; crumpled notebook paper; and an almost-empty soda bottle that really smells.

Later, Matt doesn't notice. He just jumps in and drives away, his hair still damp.

20. I find a bunch of Matt's old baseballs in our garage and put them on the Cantalonis' lawn. They'll have lots of spares now in case they hit one into the weeds.

Mrs. Millman has kept up her daily stakeouts. I find a little silver balloon in our basement, attached to a plastic stick. It has a yellow smiley face with the words HAVE A NICE DAY!

When Mrs. M. leaves for mahjong, I stick the balloon into one of her outside flowerpots (twenty-one). Maybe it will make her smile for once. But later, the balloon is gone, and notes are taped on everyone's front doors: *Important neighborhood meeting. Tonight, seven p.m. We must get to the bottom of these pranks. Yours in safety, Mrs. Myrna Millman.*

But no one can come. Conflicts, too busy.

"Probably just some kids fooling around," Dad says,

crumpling the note and tossing it into the garbage can. He shakes his head. "We had a Mrs. Millman type where I grew up. Mrs. Betty Lunetti."

"You're kidding." I laugh, sitting next to him at the kitchen counter. "You never told me that. Betty Lunetti? What a name."

"Yep. We were terrified of her. She always had these electric blue curlers in her hair, and come to think of it, she had a poodle too, this mean, yippy little dog—"

"Steven, c'mon," Mom says, opening her laptop. "Everyone knows Myrna Millman has nothing else to do except dream up this nonsense. Focus. We have to be in court first thing tomorrow."

Even though it's eight p.m., Mom looks crisp in her black trousers and sleeveless white sweater. Black-and-white-checked jacket over the back of her chair. Black heels kicked off onto the floor. You know that store that has only black-and-white clothes? Mom keeps them in business.

She's one inch shorter than me. When Matt and I were younger and she would get mad about something, we used to joke that she's four feet eleven of tough and one inch of mom.

Dad grabs his seltzer, sits down, and then flips a page on a legal pad. "Where were we?"

I want to tell them: *I like the neighborhood nonsense. It's way more fun than your nonsense.*

Mom glances at me as her phone rings. "Nina, honey. I know we haven't connected in the last few days. It's been crazy. I'll come up later. I want to hear all about the art class, okay?"

"Sure."

I fall asleep before she comes. If she even does.

The next day after summer school, when I'm getting the mail, something lightly pings the back of my head. A tiny crab apple hits the ground. I turn around. No one. I sit on the grass and flip through the envelopes; then another apple bounces off my arm.

Eli used to pull crab apples from his tree and toss them at me through the bushes that separate our side yards like a row of soldiers.

Back then it was funny. He's fourteen now, almost taller than the bushes.

"I see you," I say calmly.

He cuts through and sits next to me. "What are you doing?"

"Not much."

"I know it's you."

"What's me?"

"All this stuff that's been going on around here."

"I don't know what you're talking about."

Eli lies back, clasping his hands on his stomach. He

closes his eyes to the sun. "I've thought about it. There's no one else who would do these kinds of things. It has to be you."

I plunk the mail down. "You don't even know me anymore."

He smiles, eyes still closed. "Yes, I do."

He's teasing. He's changed. What's with him and Jorie, and the other night? I'm so mad at both of them. I mean, all this time, it was always the three of us.

I peek at Eli: the hair on his legs, his T-shirt loose around his shoulders. Faded, wrinkled cargo shorts. His fingernails: clean and short. And then, a rush of the memory of us hiding from Jorie, his brown eyes shining in the dark. My heart beating, loud and fast.

"It's okay," he says. "I won't tell anyone."

Good. Thank you.

Eli stands and walks toward his house. "My mom uses those foot things every day."

I pick up a crab apple and toss it in his direction. I've always been a good shot. The tiny apple plunks his arm.

I count this as twenty-two because he laughs.

Something that's the same: his laugh.

Eli picks up the crab apple, throws it sky-high, and then catches it. "See you later. Mystery Girl."

Jorie's mom drives us to summer school every morning. She wears cute, trendy outfits—flowy chiffon tops, skinny jeans, wedges. Each day, she sends Jorie off with some sort of caution.

"If anyone offers you drugs, just walk away."

"Don't go into the bathroom alone."

"Be sure to choose a fruit or vegetable during your snack break."

I know Jorie is aching to do the opposite. (Except for the drugs.) Every morning, though, she says sweetly, "Okay, Mom. Bye. Love you." Then she pulls my arm toward the door. Her mom watches us in the rearview mirror as she drives away.

We're early today, and Jorie sits with me on a bench by the gym. Probably because she doesn't see Savannah/Dakota/Antarctica.

The heavy girl from art, Amber, and Chase, the spike-haired guy, are sitting on a bench across from us, comparing their color wheels. They're both wearing black, head to toe. A group of jock boys walks by. One laughs and mutters, "Freaks." Amber stands, sneers, and raises a fist, but Chase pulls her arm, and they gather their stuff and leave. Jorie's oblivious, looking at her phone. Amber and Chase are halfway down the hall when I see a color wheel on the ground. Someone steps on it.

I hesitate. *Should I?* Chase picks up an empty chip bag and throws it into a can. *Yes, do it.* I bolt from the bench, grab the color wheel, and run after them. "Hey, you dropped this."

They just look at me, so I hand it to Amber. My hand is shaking a little and my heart is going a hundred miles an hour.

"Thanks," she says warily.

I nod and start walking back toward Jorie. I feel like they're watching me, but I don't look back. I say softly to myself, "Number twenty-three." This one was a little like jumping over a fence to an unfamiliar neighborhood.

Jorie's head is tipped to one side. "Why'd you do that?"

I sit. "Those color wheels, they're a big part of our grade."

"That was . . . really nice."

"It wasn't anything."

She's staring at me. "It kind of was. I wouldn't have done that. They're so weird."

"I know."

Jorie laughs. "Anyway, I was going to show you my dress." She taps her phone screen, and a strapless, shimmery, really short red dress appears.

"Your dress for what?"

"*Homecoming.* Duh."

"Wait. Did someone ask you?" Please don't say Eli. Please say someone else.

She shakes her head. "Not yet. But it's just a matter of time. A lot of girls have been asked already. The dance is so early. The middle of September."

"Oh." Not much homecoming discussion going on in art. A lot of talk about piercings, though. Where to get them, how many can go on an ear, an eyebrow, elsewhere.

"People are already talking about groups," Jorie says. "I'll have to see if Eli wants to go with my group or his. Either one's fine with me."

Eli likes her; she likes him. . . . So why is there a lump in *my* throat?

"If Eli's friend Tyler asks someone, maybe we could go with him and his older brother. How cool would that be? We wouldn't have to get our parents to drive us then."

"Right." I nod. She has it all worked out.

"If I got the red dress, which shoes would I wear? Black is always good, but it can be boring, you know? Maybe silver."

"Yeah, silver is good." My face feels hot. "Silver is *terrific*."

She flips through a few more pictures of dresses, holding up each one—turquoise, yellow, and sickening Barbie pink. "I can't even decide if that one is *the* dress. It's an important choice. It sets the tone for, like, your whole high school image, you know?" She glances at me, hesitating. She knows fashion has never been my thing. "What do you think?"

"They're all really beautiful." I look at her. *She* is beautiful. Always has been. "You'd look amazing in every single one of them." Completely true.

In my heart, I count this as number twenty-four even though it wasn't exactly anonymous.

She squeezes my arm. "Aw, thanks. Guess what? I've picked out a dress for you."

"Me?"

She shows me her phone. "Green, to go with your eyes."

"Jor, it's pretty, and of course I'd love to go to home-coming, but I don't think there's anyone who would ask me."

She stands and crosses her arms. "Leave that to me." She waves to the kids from her class, starts walking toward them. "We'll talk about this later."

"Wait, Jorie—"

She doesn't hear. She's showing her phone to Ant-arctica, then pulling her hair back, like she's describing a style. Jorie has her plan, and I have mine. How can I love and not love her at the same time?

When I get off the bus (Jorie went to Antarctica's), Mrs. Bennett is pacing in her driveway and Thomas is running around her in circles, cape on, sword in hand. She's in her royal-blue nursing scrubs and keeps checking her phone.

"Hi, Mrs. Bennett," I say. She looks completely stressed out.

"Oh, Nina." She glances up. "How are you?"

"Fine."

"Where *is* he?" she says, and sighs heavily. "Nina, could I ask a huge favor?"

"Sure."

"Eli was supposed to be home to watch Thomas by now. I have a double shift today, and I'm already late. Do you think you could keep an eye on him until Eli gets here? I know you're probably running somewhere with your friends. . . ."

Um. Not really.

"No problem," I say.

Mrs. Bennett's face lights up. "You can? You're sure?"

"Yes. It's fine. Of course."

She runs into their garage and grabs her purse, then digs inside. "I don't have a lot of cash right now. . . ."

"You don't have to pay me."

"No, that's not right."

"You said you were late. We can figure it out later."

She lets out a long breath. "You're a lifesaver." Then she catches Thomas by the arm. "Stay with Nina, okay, until Eli gets home."

"Okay!"

I take his hand while she backs the car out. He jumps and waves. "Bye, Mommy!" Then he looks up at me with the same dark brown eyes as Eli. But a lot more freckles.

"So, what do you want to do?" I ask him.

He drops my hand and marches into the garage.

"Ride!" He climbs onto a beat-up tricycle. I smile; it's Eli's. I remember when he got it and learned to pedal. He was so proud of himself. He went around the cul-de-sac about a hundred times.

I wheel Thomas to the sidewalk. He starts pedaling furiously.

"Wait! Don't cross without me!" I yell, running to catch up, although there's not a car in sight.

I walk next to him as he rides across the street, then turns left in front of the Dixon house.

He stops and points. "Scary house."

"It sure is."

He pedals to the Cantalonis'. "Baseball house."

I laugh. "Do you have a name for every house?"

He nods, serious.

"Do you ever play with the Cantalonis? Isn't the youngest kid your age?"

"Jordan? He's four. But he's always playing with his brothers."

"Oh."

Thomas points to the Millmans. "Doggie house."

Of course. The Millmans have the only pet in the neighborhood. Jorie used to have a hamster, and I had a goldfish, but well, you know how that goes. My fish didn't last long. Five-year-old traumatic experience. Dad helped me bury it in the backyard.

Thomas pedals to Mr. Dembrowski's. "Night house."

I peer at the windows. "Why night house?"

"The man there drives away in the night."

"How do you know?"

"When I dream something bad, I wake up and look out my window. Sometimes I see the man in his car."

The house looks as quiet as usual. I start imagining the worst: He's a criminal? Leads a double life? When the police finally catch him, we'll all say he used to grow flowers but we never really knew the guy. Wait—what if it's something normal, like Mr. D. works at night and sleeps during the day?

Thomas goes to Jorie's. "The funny house." He smiles and covers his mouth.

"Because?"

"The girl here is funny with Eli."

Absolutely true.

"And this one?" I gesture to Mrs. Chung's.

"The broken-leg house."

I look at the Christmas lights. "I wonder how she broke her leg."

"She falled off a ladder."

"You know everything, don't you?" I grin.

We stop at mine, and Thomas nods. He has the whole neighborhood summed up. "You are the nice house. Because you're nice."

"You're a pretty smart little guy, Thomas."

"I'm not little!"

"Sorry. So, what do you call your house?"

He gets off the tricycle and pushes his hair out of his eyes. "Mixed-up."

I kneel in front of him. "Why?"

He shakes his head. "Can't tell you."

We pull the tricycle into his garage. Eli's still not back.

"Thomas, want to go to the park?"

"Will you take me in my wagon?"

"Sure."

He climbs in, and I pull it out into the driveway. I should tell Eli, but I don't have his number. I get a sheet of paper from my sketchbook, scribble a note to him, and leave it by the door. Then I shut their garage door and run under as it's closing.

There's a pathetic little park nearby with three swings, one jungle gym, and a small climbing wall. But to Thomas, the park will be a whole new place to fight crime.

As soon as we get there, he starts making up all these complicated scenarios with bad guys and heroes, including sound effects of explosions and battles.

He's running across a bridge connecting two of the climbing towers when his cape catches on a pole and rips.

"Oh, no!" he yells. I hoist myself onto the bridge and untangle the cape. There's a gash down the center. He starts to cry.

I'm not sure what to do, but he folds into me, and I'm hugging him and stroking his soft hair. "It's okay."

"No, it's not." He pulls away. "You can't fight bad guys with a broken cape," he says sadly.

"What if I know someone who can fix the cape?"

He wipes his cheek with the back of his hand. "Who?"

"Just someone. Will you let me borrow it?"

He blinks. "Maybe."

"C'mon. Let's head back."

Thomas gets into the wagon, broken cape and all. He looks up at me. "But what can I use when it's fixing?"

"We'll think of something."

When we get back, Eli still isn't there. My stomach flutters. What if something happened to him?

Thomas comes into my house, and while he's busy matching his foot to Matt's size-eleven shoe, I untie the cape from around his neck. Even I have to admit, he doesn't look right without it. I find an old pillow-case and tie it loosely around Thomas's neck. He seems satisfied. Then he lets out one of those exhausted kid breaths, goes over to our sofa, and falls asleep.

There are so many good things to count today.

25. Watched Thomas. 26. Took him to the park. 27. Comforted him. 28. Found a replacement cape.

I'm way ahead.

My grandma taught me to sew. Simple Truth: Sewing comes in handy.

To me, Grandma was this plump, sweet old lady who showed me how to wet the thread in my mouth so it's easier to slip through the eye of the needle. But to Mom, she was a constant aggravation. They never got along. How could they, a content homemaker and a tough divorce attorney? They were like two opposite ends of the history of women. Maybe Mom was adopted and never told anyone.

She kept Grandma's sewing basket, though. This

gives me hope that Mom loved her mother in some small way. It's way back in a kitchen cabinet; hasn't been used in a long time. When I take it out, it's like Grandma is in the room. The basket is filled with stuff no one else I know has—shiny silver thimbles, lace wound around a cardboard wheel, a rainbow of thread colors, different-size needles stuck in the pincushion on the inside lid. And the buttons. A whole removable top tray of them. They're fascinating to me; simple but so essential. Small and round. Fabric, metal, plastic. Two holes, four holes, and some with a little hook under the button, which is the hardest to sew.

Mom never uses the basket. If she needs pants hemmed or a button sewed on, she drops the clothes off at the cleaners. Grandma told me she tried to teach Mom to sew when she was little, but Mom didn't have the patience for it.

I look over at Thomas, still sound asleep. There's a wet spot on the sofa where he drooled.

I get a needle ready with black thread and spread the cape across my lap. I knot the end of the thread and pull the needle through the fabric, hiding the knot on the inside. Then, small, even stitches, like Grandma showed me. In, out, again. I work my way up the rip, and it slowly mends with every stitch. I have to stop for a second as I remember Grandma sitting in her armchair, sewing, a carrot ring in the oven. Nutmeg.

Brown sugar. Cinnamon. The smells filling her apartment. ST: Carrots are good for the eyes. And the heart.

We went there a lot for Sunday dinners. For me, it was like being wrapped in a soft, warm blanket. Dad and Matt were always thrilled. Grandma was a good cook. But Mom always had her lips pressed together the whole time. While we drove home, she'd comment on things Grandma had said, or hadn't said, or should have said, and I didn't get any of it.

When I'm done sewing, I tie a small double knot in the thread and hold up the cape. It looks like it has a scar. I hope Thomas will be okay with it.

He breathes through his mouth as he sleeps. His cheeks are pink, and his eyelashes are a little clumped together from the crying. I rub his back softly. His skin feels warm through the pillowcase. He makes a sound, a hum-sigh. For the first time in my life, I feel a little motherly.

Number twenty-nine.

This was a huge day.

I close the sewing basket. When Grandma got weak, she stopped being able to do normal things by herself. Like write. Hold a spoon. The worst was when she couldn't sew anymore.

I don't know I'm crying until a tear drops onto the pillowcase.

14

Eli comes to pick up Thomas but doesn't say where he was. He seems angry and brushes past me. Maybe I shouldn't ask questions, but I can't help it.

"Are you okay?"

He flashes me a look, then goes over to the sofa and gently shakes Thomas's shoulder.

I follow him. "I mean, your mom was worried."

He turns around. He looks sweaty, and his elbow has a raw scrape on it, like it just stopped bleeding a few minutes ago. "I'm *fine.*"

"Really?"

"Yeah." He grabs the cape and scoops up Thomas, who is groggy. "*Yeah*. I am. Okay?"

"Sure." I glance at his elbow, and I'm sure he sees.

Eli walks to the door, Thomas in his arms. Eli looks like a dad at that moment, Thomas's head on his shoulder, a little hand clutching Eli's white T-shirt, legs dangling by Eli's waist. I realize how much I like this about Eli. How good he is with Thomas. How protective. The big brother everyone needs.

"You don't have to worry about me," Eli says sharply. "*Okay?*"

I untie the pillowcase and slide it off Thomas's neck. "Okay."

"Thanks for watching him."

"No problem."

I watch Eli walk toward his house, carrying Thomas and the cape, like he's trying to hold it all together. He definitely needs someone to worry about him.

My house feels lonely without Thomas sleeping on the sofa. I get one of my summer reading books, *The Alchemist,* read the first five pages, and become thoroughly confused. I hear Matt's door open. I didn't even know he was home.

He comes bounding down the stairs, takes off his headphones. "Hey. What's up?"

"Nothing." I put the book down. "Everything."

Surprise. He sits next to me on the sofa.

"You look the way you looked when your goldfish died," he says.

"I do?"

He points to the book. "I remember this. Never understood it."

"Oh, great."

"Hey, I owe you a card game, don't I?"

"Don't you have to go somewhere? Work?"

"In a half hour." Matt goes into the kitchen, grabs a deck from the drawer, and then comes back and starts shuffling it. Fast and neat, like a pro.

"When did you get so good at shuffling?"

He shrugs, starts dealing. "War?"

"Okay. I'm going to beat you this time."

He laughs, and in about fifteen minutes, I'm down to a couple of twos and fours and one lonely king.

"I don't get how you always win," I groan. "Do you have some secret strategy?"

He stretches his arms out, wiggles his fingers. "I'm just lucky."

A few more cards, one last war, and we're done.

"That was the fastest game of war ever," I say. I search Matt's face. This is the first time we've played since Grandma died. Doesn't he remember what happened?

Hard to tell. These days, he keeps everything inside.

He shuffles the deck. "You know how to play poker?"

"Uh-uh. No one ever showed me."

"*What?* That has to change."

He deals, puts the rest of the deck on the table, turns the top card over. "We'll play open hand. So, what you want to do is look for things like pairs, straights."

"I have two queens."

"That's pretty good."

"Wait. What do you have? Did I possibly beat you, for once in my life?"

He looks at his cards, smiles. "Yeah. You did. Not bad for someone who's never played poker before." Matt glances at the clock. "Oh, man, I gotta go." He stands, looks at me for a long second.

"What?"

"This was fun." I think he's going to say something else, but he's out the door. In the Jeep. Evaporated.

The pool closes at seven. Where does he go after? Please tell me it's nothing like when he got in trouble at school.

Later, when Mom and Dad come in and spread out at the table, I sit down with them. Other parents might get it, that maybe I want to talk. That maybe this is a small yet momentous gesture from their teenage child.

Hello, I'm here. But they barely look up. Just a few scattered words.

Dad: "Everything okay?"

Mom: "Your hair's getting long. You could use a trim."

"So how's the case going?" I ask them.

"Just . . . one . . . sec," Dad says, flipping through a legal pad. Then to Mom: "We have to go after the Florida property."

"Of course."

"Heck, Bermuda too," Dad says, and laughs.

Mom nods. "Not that we'll get it."

I pour myself some lemonade and move to a stool at the island. "Matt taught me how to play poker. Wanna play when you're done?"

Dad hands a file to Mom. "Sure, in a bit."

"You're done reading this?" Mom asks him.

"Pokerrr," I say, swirling my lemonade as I spin on the stool.

Dad smiles. "You used to spin like that when you were little and didn't like what we were having for dinner."

Mom writes something. "Nina, honey, just a minute—"

"Oh, am I interrupting the lawyer show?"

She takes off her reading glasses, looks at me. Finally.

"We're not ignoring you; we're just so preoccupied. The media are all over this case. You wouldn't believe what's been going on. It's incredibly exciting—the kind of case I've wanted all these years."

"It's like being on top of a mountain," Dad says.

Yeah.

Mom crosses her legs, starts speed-talking, making up for lost time. "How's the art class? How are your friends from the basketball team? Jorie's good? We'll have lunch when this is all wrapped up, okay? You'll catch me up." She's tapping her fingernails on the table. "We can go to the mall. You can get some cute new outfits for school."

"People don't wear *outfits*, Mom."

She gives me a quick smile. "You know what I mean."

"Sure."

She picks up her phone. "Matt didn't text me back."

"He's eighteen. What do you expect?" Dad shrugs. "He'll be away at college next month. Get used to it."

Mom stands and stretches her arms overhead. I don't know how she even spots this, being so *preoccupied* and all, but she creases her brows and her lips pinch into a thin line. "Why is that out?"

The sewing basket is on the counter. Big mistake.

"I needed to sew something today," I say lightly, then get up and return it to the cabinet. It's gone. But still, Erica Fine doesn't look fine. She makes a fist. Her polished red nails dig into her skin. Ow.

"Every time I see that thing," she says, "that floral print *basket,* there's my mother, in her dull print dress, sitting in her armchair, *sewing.*"

I want to say, *What's wrong with that?* But I pretty much know Mom's answer.

Here it is.

She imitates Grandma's voice. "Every girl should know how to sew, Erica." She plunks back into her chair. "Who knows where I'd be if I'd listened to her."

Dad glances at Mom, then turns to me. "What were you sewing?"

"Just something."

He smiles. "I think it's nice that you can sew. Not many girls do that anymore."

Mom takes a sip of water, then sets the bottle down hard. It tips over, and water floods their papers.

"Oh, that's just great!" she yells.

I run for the paper towels.

Dad blots the papers with one hand. He puts the other hand on Mom's arm. "Are you okay?"

"Absolutely fine."

"Erica, when this case is over, we should take my brother up on his offer to use their cabin. Get away for a few days."

Mom balls up the paper towels, throws them out. "I can't think about that right now."

They look at each other, and I suddenly feel like I should leave. "I guess I'll go upstairs."

Mom pats me on the arm. Dad blows me a kiss.

They were never big huggers, like Jorie's parents. At least I used to get a bedtime story—Dad reading in funny voices, Mom brushing the tangles from my hair. But I grew up, and things happen. Things change.

In my room, I start to lower the shade, then stop to study Mr. Dembrowski's house. It looks the same.

The houses in the cul-de-sac are mostly dark. A few lights on in scattered rooms, the blue flicker from a TV. That big tree by the Millmans' swaying in the night breeze. A piece of paper blowing around in the Cantalonis' yard. Shirts from the dry cleaner's hanging in a plastic bag on Jorie's front door.

Then I see a flash of light from the Dixon house.

Someone's in there?

The realtor? Burglars? . . . The *kumiho*?

The light seems to move around a little, then goes out. I watch for a few minutes, my heart racing. The Dixon house stays dark.

When I can finally tear myself from the window, I do an online search for *"kumiho."* The word literally means "nine-tailed fox." There are different versions of the Korean legend. Most say a *kumiho* is a fox that has lived for a thousand years, has nine tails, and can turn into a beautiful but evil woman. Sometimes a *kumiho* tricks a man into marriage. Or they lurk in the forest, eating men's livers.

Nice. I hope that isn't a bedtime story for kids in Korea.

Nowhere, however, does it say that a *kumiho* has the power to turn on a light in a vacant house.

In art the next day, we finish our abstract clay pieces so they can get fired. Abstract is good; no one has to guess what mine is. Then we have to find a partner. Which is an awful thing that teachers do. Are they unable to see how this goes? The people who know each other pair up in a second (Amber and Chase, the two girls I knew in junior high), and then there are random floaters avoiding each other.

I'm a floater.

Swallow. Look around. Brief moment of panic. Then, relief. Sariah and I make eye contact. Which is helpful, because the assignment is to draw each other's eye. Hers are dark brown and make me think of a chocolate fountain. I'm glad to see that she has normal piercings, just on her earlobes.

Sariah and I face each other, desk to desk, holding our sketchpads. In less than ten minutes, she has drawn my eye in complete detail, including the lid and lashes.

"How'd you do that so fast?" I ask. I'm still on the outline. Sariah doesn't even have a pupil yet.

She shrugs.

"You're good," I say.

"Thanks."

"That's really what my eye looks like?"

She nods, still filling in the sketch.

She's drawn an eye that's almond-shaped and lazy, with long lashes and little flecks where the green is. Maybe there is something about me that is actually sort of beautiful.

Time for the break. I start cleaning up my supplies. One of my pencils rolls off the desk and across the floor, like it's running away. A boot stops it. Chase picks it up, holds it out.

There's this odd second when we look at each other and he's holding one end of the pencil and I'm holding the other.

I tuck the pencil into my bag. "Thanks."

Chase smiles. He has a chipped front tooth. *"De nada."*

Small thing. But big, too.

Today, Sariah and I sit on the risers in the commons. I feel very short. "How tall are you?"

She smiles down with a mouth full of silver braces. "Five eight."

Jorie hasn't noticed I'm not there. A guy with long plaid shorts grabs her water bottle and throws it to another guy. She tries to get it (jumping high so her shirt goes up and her bare tan stomach shows), but they're tossing it around. She sits down and crosses her arms and pretends to pout; then the plaid guy brings it to her. Pouting works, at least for Jorie. He kneels in front of her, like he's asking for forgiveness. I can hear her laugh all the way over here as she ruffles his hair.

Wait. What about Eli? Why is she flirting with that guy? I don't get her sometimes.

"So, anyway," I say, and turn to Sariah. She's unwrapping a cookie and taking miniature bites around the edges.

I find out she went to a different junior high. She dances. Giggles a lot. She collects frogs, little glass and plastic and metal figurines. "I have a hundred and two," she says.

"Wow. That's a lot of frogs."

"Uh-huh. I have two whole frog shelves in my room." She brushes cookie crumbs from her fingers. "Did you know frogs don't drink water but they absorb it through their skin?"

"I didn't know that." I laugh and sort of poke her. "This is getting weird."

But she's completely serious. "Frogs are fascinating. Some scientists think frog juice can cure diseases."

I raise my eyebrows. "Frog juice?"

She nods. "Chemicals in their skin. People might be able to make medicines from them."

Okay then.

"Did you know there are thousands of species of frogs in the world?"

"Um, no."

Out of the corner of my eye, I see Jorie sitting on plaid guy's lap, laughing hysterically. Her real laugh, not the fake one she did with Eli. I feel a pain in my stomach.

"Cookie?" Sariah offers.

I pull an apple from my bag. "No, thanks."

Sariah looks away. Maybe I've hurt her feelings, not being so interested in frogs. But c'mon, it's a little strange.

I touch her arm. "Your drawings are amazing. You're really talented."

She smiles. "Thanks."

Number thirty.

Jorie laughs; Sariah chews. It feels like I've crossed over to the other side of something. And I'm not sure it feels right. But the other side didn't either. So where am I supposed to go?

16

Two people have told me I'm an old soul. Mr. Pontello and Grandma.

It's not as creepy as it sounds.

An "old soul" is a spiritual person who is wise beyond her years. A soul who has lived before. A person who sees everything in the universe as part of one great interwoven tapestry.

First, Mr. Pontello. There were times when he'd be lecturing about World War II or Vietnam, and I got things on a deeper level, more than just the facts and figures we needed to know for the test. People fell asleep in his class and laughed at his cowboy boots and buzz cut, but he made me love history. Showed me how we can learn from our mistakes. On my last essay of the year, Mr. Pontello wrote in the margin, *You are an old soul.*

Grandma told me when she taught me how to sew. She said she could tell by my stitches.

She said they were too even and steady for a young person and I was much too comfortable with a needle and thread.

"But I'm only ten," I said.

"Don't worry." She peered closely at a tablecloth she was repairing. "It's a good thing. A very good thing."

"I don't get it."

"You will one day. Something will happen."

Old souls, she explained, may not be the most light-hearted people in a room, but their hearts have the kind of light that stays on for a long time.

That sounded a little scary. It made me think of E.T.'s glowing red heart.

But now I think I'm getting it. I wish I could tell her. Something happened the day I planted Mrs. Chung's marigolds.

When I get off the bus, Mr. Millman is helping Mrs. Cantaloni carry in the grocery bags piled in the back of her minivan.

I stand in the middle of the street and watch Mr. Millman pick up two bags in each hand and follow Mrs. Cantaloni inside. She's getting so big, she waddles. He comes back out for the rest of the bags, whistling.

Wait. Whistling? Are my little efforts rubbing off on someone else? Maybe doing good is contagious, like stares.

Perhaps for Mr. Millman, but not Mrs. Millman. She's standing in her driveway, holding Beanie on a tight leash, tapping her beige loafer. When Mr. Millman finishes with the bags, he walks toward her, and she says, "I can't remember the last time you helped *me* with the groceries."

"Is it my fault you do the shopping when I'm at the office?"

"And what's with the cigars all of a sudden?" she snaps. "You're going to get tongue cancer."

Mr. Millman stamps his foot. "Myrna, live a little."

"I live just fine, thank you very much!"

All this time, Beanie's been pulling at the leash, sniffing something in the air. Suddenly, she breaks free and bolts into the Dixon weeds.

Mrs. Chung starts coming down her driveway, swinging the crutches fast.

The weeds are moving where Beanie must be nosing through them. Mrs. Millman runs to the edge. "Beanie, darling! Come out of there right now!" She stands on her tiptoes. "Stan! Do something!"

"What do you want me to do?" He has a little smile. I think he's enjoying this.

Mrs. Chung reaches Mrs. Millman just as Beanie darts out of the weeds, howling with that awful hurt dog sound.

"She's bleeding!" Mrs. Millman shrieks.

I knew this was coming.

"*Kumiho.*" Mrs. Chung nods. "Fox in those weeds. She waits. Watches."

"What are you talking about?" Mrs. Millman says, scooping up Beanie, who's yelping in pain. "Stan! Take me to the vet! *Something* bit Beanie! That place is a menace!"

He motions toward their garage. "C'mon!"

Thomas, in his driveway, raises his sword. Jack Cantaloni and his brothers run out as the Millmans leap into their car and back out of their driveway. Mrs. Chung is staring at the weeds, nodding.

In a second, the Cantaloni boys have hit a baseball into the weeds. Haven't they figured out how to hit closer pop-ups? But then the balls would land in Mrs. Millman's yard. What a choice. Weeds with a *kumiho* or the crazy woman of the neighborhood.

Mrs. Chung turns and starts toward her house. "Bad sign." The boys just stare at her.

We need a good thing. This very minute.

I approach Mrs. Chung. "Some legends say foxes are wise and can be faithful guardians," I tell her. "You know, watch over everyone."

"Where did you hear that?"

"I read it on the Internet."

"And so you believe it?" She shuffles away.

Well, I tried.

"Can you get the ball?" Jack asks me. "Did you see where it landed?"

"Yeah." I find the ball and toss it to him. What could have bitten Beanie? I don't see or hear anything. Maybe a spider.

Jordan tosses his mitt into the air. Jack says, "Thanks" and nudges the middle brother. "Jeremy, outfield. I'm batting. Jordan, you pitch."

Thomas is still in his driveway.

"Hey, guys, so who's catching?" I ask.

Jack shrugs. "We don't have a catcher."

"Thomas?" I wave. "They need a catcher."

He walks over, hesitant.

Jack sizes him up. "Can you catch?"

Thomas puts down his sword. "Yeah."

"Okay." Jack points. "Stand right there."

Thomas's brown eyes are shining. Thirty-one.

18

The tiny flame in my heart is getting stronger.

32. I use $2.17 of my own money to buy a tasty-looking bone for Beanie. That poor dog was definitely bitten by something, *and* she has to live with Mrs. Millman. I leave it on their front step.

33. I wrap up two slices of banana bread in foil and drop them off at Mr. Dembrowski's. Mrs. Bennett made a loaf for me as a thank-you for watching Thomas that day. No one's been eating it except me.

34. Mom has about fifteen unopened bottles of lotion in her bathroom, a miniature beauty supply

warehouse. She can't possibly use all of these. I wrap one with a ribbon and give it to Jack Cantaloni.

"I think your mom could use a foot rub," I tell him. Mr. C. always gets home late, and travels a lot for his job.

Jack looks at me like I'm as crazy as Mrs. Millman. He unscrews the top, sniffs it, and then squeezes the bottle. A big glop of lotion squirts out and lands on his shoes.

"Yuck," he says. It's all over his hands, too.

Backfire.

"Maybe I should take that back," I say.

He hands it to me and heads inside, shouting, "Mom? My shoes are full of smelly girl stuff!"

Does an attempt still count?

Speaking of Mrs. Millman—Beanie has been wearing one of those dog lampshade cone things. She had to be shaved on her back and get five stitches after what Mrs. Millman calls "the attack." She contacted an animal control service, but since there's no one living in the Dixon house, they said they couldn't set a trap without permission.

Eli hasn't been around much. But Jorie is zooming ahead with her homecoming plan. She asks me to go to the mall with her. "I want to show you the dress," she says. I think she had a fight with Antarctica.

Jorie's mom drops us off. "Don't leave your purse in

a dressing room if you go out to get a different size," she says as we get out of the car.

Jorie rolls her eyes, which are pale blue, like faded jeans. "Bye, Mom. Love you." She tucks her arm through mine and lets out a contented sigh. "I love the mall."

I laugh. She's in her second home.

We go into this store with way-too-loud music and a fake-friendly girl handing out coupons and spritzing us with perfume. Jorie takes a dozen dresses into a room. Colors called Morocco and Miami. (Red and yellow.) Jorie comes out and models them for me.

"How would I wear my hair with this one? What about shoes? What goes with yellow? The red one makes me look like I have more on top, don't you think? Do you know Eli's favorite color? The boy has to match his tie to the girl's dress. I probably should eliminate Miami. Eli wouldn't want to wear a yellow tie."

"Are you going to let me answer, Jor?" I smile at her in the mirror.

"Which is your favorite?"

My nails still have little bits of the light pink polish she did weeks ago. I hold them up. "I'm pink; you're red."

"You're absolutely right. I just want to try on that purple one. . . ." She goes back into the dressing room.

I walk around the store, trying to avoid the perfume girl (who doesn't remember she already sprayed me), and I see Sariah, with a woman who must be her mom.

Uh-oh. I don't want to hear any more about frogs. And if I say hi and Jorie sees us talking, I know she'll do that half smile with the corner of her lips pulled up. A *Who's she?* smile. I morph into not such a nice person, pretending to be absorbed in a rack of tank tops.

This erases, like, ten good things.

Luckily, Sariah and her mom leave the store, and I don't think she saw me. Or if she did, maybe she also spotted Jorie coming my way in a ruffly purple dress (Maui) and got it.

Then I see it. A dress. I pull it out. Blue. Not even really blue, more like a hint of the lightest blue you could ever imagine. I have to summon vocabulary words to describe it. Words like "gossamer" and "ethereal." If I was going to homecoming, I wouldn't have to try on a dozen dresses. This would be it. If I got asked. Which is unlikely. Closer to impossible.

On the way home, in the backseat of her mom's car, Jorie turns to me. "I have a serious question. Why do you never text me back? Are you ignoring me or something?"

"It's my phone. It's possessed. Texts don't always come through."

"Nina Ross. How can you live without a phone? Sometimes I just do not *get* you."

I know.

"But," she says, leaning her head on my shoulder, "I love you."

I know.

"Remember at camp, when we jumped off the cliff together into that freezing lake?" she says.

"Together? You made me."

"I had to! That was the only way you were going to jump!"

"We screamed the whole way."

Hitting the water, I thought I was going to drown. I plummeted so deep into the shocking cold that I thought, *This is how I'm going to die.* Jorie grabbed my arm and pulled me to the shore. Then brought me my towel. Wrapped me up and rubbed my back until my teeth stopped chattering.

She lifts her head. "It was fun that day. One of our best times."

"Jor." I blink back a tear, then lean against her.

She takes my hand.

For a split second of our lives, we are right there with each other.

"I love you too," I whisper.

She closes her eyes. "It's hard. So much effort. Being *on* all the time . . ."

I think about her seventh birthday party. And now her new group. The guy with the plaid shorts throwing her water bottle.

"Then don't do it," I say. "Just be yourself. Remember, everyone else is already taken."

Jorie shakes her head. "But I want to."

We turn into the cul-de-sac, and the moment evaporates.

"Look!" Jorie squeals.

Eli's shooting baskets in his driveway. No shirt on.

"Oh my God," she breathes.

I have to agree.

"Mom, let us out." Jorie unbuckles and scoots forward. Her mom stops, and Jorie tumbles out the door. "Hey!" she calls, in a voice that gives "hey" a whole new meaning.

Do I follow? Sit in the car? No rack of tank tops to hide behind.

"Are you getting out?" Jorie's mom asks.

"Um."

"I'll pull into our garage," she offers.

"Okay. Thank you."

I think that was a good thing from her. In some weird way.

"I like your shirt today," I tell her. "That color looks really good on you."

She smiles at me in the rearview mirror. "Really? I wondered if it was a little too young for me."

"No, it's cute."

She gets out of the car and squeezes my arm. "Thanks for noticing."

Okay, that's number thirty-five.

I'm more than halfway to my goal of sixty-five good things. Some of them haven't been exactly anonymous, but who says I can't change the rules midway? It's my plan, right?

I'm walking toward my house, trying not to look at Jorie and Eli, when Thomas runs up in his scarred cape. I kneel, and he practically knocks me over with his fierce hug.

"The cape still works okay?" I ask.

"Yeah! But who fixed it?"

I grin at him. "Someone I know with special powers."

If only this was true, then I could fix a lot more things.

"Who?" he demands.

"A person who tries to be good," I whisper. "And fight off enemies, just like you." He nods. "So are you catching a lot of criminals?"

He makes a muscle. "Yep! Lots of bad guys around here. But I'm tough!"

I feel his upper arm. "You sure are." Out of the corner of my eye I see Jorie softly punch Eli's bare stomach. He grabs her little fist, and she fake yells, "Ow!"

Well.

"I'm going home, Thomas. I'll see you later, okay?"

"Don't go!" he cries. "Want to help me kill the bad guys?"

I shake my head. "You don't want to kill them. Just put them in jail, right?"

He frowns, then motions for me to come closer. He cups his mouth with his hand and whispers, "Eli says Daddy has to give Mommy some money or else he might go to jail!"

I look at Eli. What's going on?

"Daddy comes over. Mommy and Daddy fight. Daddy goes away. Eli tries to find him and get the money."

Oh.

I pick Thomas up, and he cries a little on my shoulder. I carry him back to his mixed-up house and set him down on the grass.

"Thanks," Eli says, ruffling Thomas's hair.

"Nina," Jorie says, laughing. "You're such a mom!"

Thomas is up in a second, leaping through the air, his cape streaming behind him.

Eli smiles as Thomas slashes a bush with his sword. He glances at me. "So you sewed his cape, right? That day you watched him?"

"Yeah."

"He kept asking me how it got fixed. I finally told him it was this new superhero called Mystery Girl. He loved that."

"My secret identity."

"Something everyone should have," Eli says, and nods.

"I don't get it." Jorie looks from Eli to me. "What are you guys talking about?"

Eli picks up the basketball.

"Tell me!" Jorie begs.

Eli shoots the ball. He's got a few curls of hair on his chest. Where did those come from? I don't know if I'm grossed out or fascinated.

"Okay," Jorie says. "Don't tell me."

Eli tosses me the ball, and I catch it. "Two on one?" he says, raising an eyebrow, looking from me to Jorie.

Another thing I can do besides sew—shoot a basketball. Matt taught me. The distance from the edge of our grass to our basket is about the same as the distance in Eli's driveway. I back up, bouncing the ball.

Jorie puts her hands on her hips. "You can't make it from there. Anyway, Eli's been showing me how to do a layup."

Eli tips his chin. "Go ahead, Neen."

Swish.

He bounces the ball back to me. "Shoot till you miss."

I make four more; then the ball hits the rim.

"Okay, my turn," Jorie sings.

"I gotta go anyway," I say.

"You sure?" Eli grins. "Jorie could *definitely* use your help."

Jorie gives him a little push. "Shut up."

I start walking toward my house. "It's okay. You guys play. I have to do something for art that's due tomorrow."

"Nina!" Eli shouts.

I turn back. I'm on my grass. Eli chucks me the ball. "Try it."

"From here?"

"No way," Jorie says.

I focus on the basket. This would be the shot of a lifetime. I heave the ball with all my strength, like I'm doing the shot put or something. It misses by several feet.

Jorie grabs the ball. "I knew you weren't *that* good."

I turn, head toward my front door.

"Nice try, though," Eli calls.

"Hey, Eli," I hear Jorie say. "What's your favorite color?"

I stop.

"I don't know. Blue?" he says.

Sunset that night. I'm sitting on our front step, thinking how much the colors look like Mrs. Chung's marigolds, which have grown and spread. They look like
marigolds on steroids. Must be the magical work of the
kumiho.

I'm trying not to think about Jorie and Eli.

The Cantaloni boys are out as usual, playing baseball, but this time, Thomas is with them. "Can you
pitch?" Jack asks him. Thomas nods and puts down
his sword. Their four outlines are silhouetted against
the orange and gold sky.

Jack looks my way. "If the ball goes into the weeds, will you get it, Nina?"

"Sure!"

Matt drives up, parks the Jeep in front of our house. He's in his bathing suit, a towel around his shoulders. He gets out and shakes his wet hair.

He spots me. "What're you doing?"

I shrug. "Just sitting."

He takes off the towel and pretends to snap it at me. "How's *The Alchemist* going?"

"Not good."

"I can give you my old notes. Except"—he laughs—"I got a C in that class."

"Sure. Why not?"

"Okay, I gotta shower." He walks past me, opens the door. "Hey, you should come to the pool sometime. I could get you in for free."

Who would I go with? I think about Jorie, Eli, Sariah, and my old group, who are supposed to be back soon. I'm in between everything.

"Maybe."

Matt goes inside as Jack hits the ball. It flies into the weeds. "Nina!" he shouts. I run over and look but can't find it. "I think this one's gone, guys."

Jack gets another ball from their garage. "You're like our camp counselor."

"Yeah!" Thomas grins. "Camp Nina!"

"Can you play the outfield?" Jack asks me.

I smile and back up toward the Millmans'. "I'll cover left."

Thirty-six?

We play a while, and when it's dark, their moms call them inside. I'm walking home, and I see something stuck to the side of our mailbox. I didn't notice it before—a folded piece of plain white paper. It's a note, in small, neat printing. It says, *Thank you.—Les Dembrowski.*

So much for being anonymous.

I tuck the note into my pocket, then climb into the hammock and stretch out. Let me just review here. Mrs. Chung was elated with the marigolds, Mr. Millman and Mrs. Cantaloni are buds, Mrs. Bennett uses the foot pads every day, Mr. Millman enjoys cigars, Thomas is playing with the Cantaloni boys *and* continues to fight neighborhood crime with his repaired cape. Mr. Dembrowski is well fed, and thankful.

I unfold Mr. D.'s note and read it again, then look around at our Fertile Crescent on a starry summer night.

Mrs. Millman is right about this. *Something* is going on in this neighborhood.

Because of me.

21

Sariah must have seen me in the store at the mall. She's avoiding me in art. I brought her a cup of water for rinsing her paintbrushes when I got one for myself, but she didn't even look up. I said hi a few times, but she acted like she didn't hear.

The thing is, I'm not even sure I want to be friends with her. She doesn't know me like Jorie does . . . that I'm scared of deep water or I'm "such a mom" or I have a habit of dropping phones.

At the breaks, I'm back to sitting on the edge of Jorie's group.

Mrs. Cantaloni is now huge. How can skin stretch that much? Being pregnant looks painful. I'd like to give Jack another bottle of lotion, but Mom might notice something is missing. Plus he'd probably make it explode again.

37. I feel bad for Mrs. Bennett, now that Thomas told me about their dad. Those gel shoe pads are good for her feet but don't help with the big picture. Not that this will either, but I find a ceramic flowerpot in our basement, dig up a few of Mrs. Chung's marigolds, plant them in the pot, and leave it on Mrs. Bennett's doorstep.

38. I put a note in Mr. Dembrowski's mailbox: *You're welcome*. I don't need to sign it.

I have something big planned for number forty. I've been thinking about it for a while. It's something I should have done a long time ago. Actually, something me, Jorie, and Eli should have done, but now that they're practically a couple, I'll just do it myself. Which is okay. Sort of.

Art goes extra slowly today. (We're working on perspective and vanishing points.) Then, finally, Jorie and I are walking to the buses. A silver minivan pulls up, and the door slides open. Eli calls, "Want a ride?" Two guys are in the front seats.

Jorie takes off, running unsteadily in her wedges, tote bag bouncing against her hip. "Absolutely! Nina, come on!" Before I reach the car, she plops herself into the middle seat next to Eli. I climb into the way back like a little kid.

"You know Tyler." Eli gestures. "And this is his brother, Sam."

Jorie stands, leans toward the front seat, and turns up the music. She chatters, texts Antarctica, puts on lip gloss, flirts. I can't get a word in, even if I could think of something funny or cute.

I sit back, let the wind blow my hair, and look at Eli's hand on the armrest. Which Jorie keeps touching.

At Eli's house, Tyler and Sam get out; Jorie tumbles out, almost falls. The boys grab a basketball and start shooting. Eli stays in his seat and looks back at me, tips his head toward their front step. "She loved the flowers."

I smile.

"She thought it was me and Thomas, and we didn't exactly tell her it wasn't. She said it felt like Mother's Day or something."

I climb into the middle seat next to him. He leans a little closer. "She was mad at me. I forgot to do some stuff, like the laundry. She calmed down when she saw the flowers." His hair grazes my cheek. "You saved me. It's like you knew."

"What are you guys doing in there?" Jorie calls, looking at her phone.

I have this crazy, completely insane feeling that Eli wants to kiss me. But (1) Am I out of my mind? And (2) Jorie is standing at the car door.

"Oh my God," she says, and giggles. "Dakota got asked to homecoming! You know that boy Dylan? The one with red hair? Anyway, he made a bouquet out of those Dum Dum lollipops with a card that said 'D and D isn't dum. Let's pop over to homecoming together.' Is that the cutest thing you ever heard?" She holds up the picture on her phone—the lollipop creation.

"Very cute," Eli says.

"Creative," I agree.

"Now, me"—Jorie bats her eyes—"I prefer chocolate."

"She likes chocolate, dude," Sam teases, passes the ball to Tyler.

"Good to know." Eli laughs, and my heart drops seventeen miles as we get out. He goes over to the driveway and starts shooting.

Jorie's practically drooling, staring at the boys.

Thomas flings open the front door. "Eli! Mom needs you!"

"Okay. In a minute," Eli says, running past Tyler for a layup. Thomas waves to me. "Camp Nina today?"

I laugh. "Maybe!"

The boys say they have to go, and Eli rolls the ball into their garage.

"Wait!" Jorie runs over, pulls him close, and holds her phone out. She takes a picture. "I'm sending this to Dakota right now. It's *so* sweet!"

Eli runs up his front steps, and Jorie starts walking backward toward her house. "You think he got the hint?" She grins. "About the chocolate?"

"Yeah, I think so."

"I'm so excited! It's almost a done deal."

"Seems like it."

"And, Neens, I haven't forgotten about you. I'm working on it." Her phone rings. "Oh my God," she shouts into it. "Let me tell you what just happened."

She reaches her house. Her voice sails through the sticky summer air.

"Jorie," I whisper, watching her. I miss the girl who couldn't glue, brought me the towel after we jumped into the water, made sure I was okay. The girl I knew.

22

The next day, Mrs. Millman and Mrs. Chung are standing on the sidewalk. Mrs. M. reports that Beanie is suffering from post-traumatic stress syndrome. Although the vet wasn't sure exactly what kind of animal bit her, she had to get some shots, and that put her over the edge. So says the dog psychologist.

Mrs. Millman is counting Beanie's symptoms off on her fingers. With each one, Mrs. Chung nods, as if that's exactly what she would expect after an encounter with a *kumiho*.

"Whimpering. Cowering under furniture. Trembling

at the slightest noise. Loss of appetite. Lethargic. Won't come outside. And worst of all, my beloved Beanie will no longer cuddle with me and watch *Dancing with the Stars*. It was her favorite show. I don't know if she'll ever return to her old self."

Mrs. Chung shakes her head. "Such a shame."

Mrs. Millman turns and looks at the Dixon house. "Since the authorities won't help, it is my duty to deal with whatever's lurking in those weeds."

"Not easy. The fox is smart. Full of surprises."

"I read that animals don't like the scent of certain strong spices," Mrs. Millman says.

"On the Internet?"

"Yes."

"Ha!"

Mrs. Millman crosses her arms. "I have a plan."

Mrs. Chung raises her eyebrows.

"Paprika."

"Hmm."

"Tabasco?"

"Won't work."

"What about mothballs?"

Mrs. Chung holds her nose.

"Well!" Mrs. Millman straightens her shoulders. "I'm going to give it a try. It's all I can do. Perhaps if I can drive away the animal in there, Beanie will be able to live without fear."

"You waste some good spices." The ever doubtful Mrs. Chung starts making her way back to her house. She waves at me. Just as she reaches her driveway, a car pulls up and a young man and woman get out. Her kids. I haven't seen them in a long time. I'm so happy they're visiting; she needs company. And a distraction.

Later, I spot Mrs. Millman in her buttoned-up cardigan and loafers, holding a big jar of reddish powder and sprinkling it into the weeds. Then she walks around with two bottles of Tabasco, pouring out some sauce every few feet. She tosses in a few mothballs and shouts, "Let's see how you like that!"

She goes inside to watch from the window, as if she's expecting the cause of Beanie's distress to come running out of the weeds immediately. Doesn't happen.

Matt drives up, windows open, music blasting, and parks right over the oil spot.

"Hi," I call.

He gets out. "What's that smell?"

"Paprika. Tabasco sauce. Mothballs."

"Huh?"

I walk toward him, my bare toes deep in the grass. "Long story. It's pretty funny, actually, although there's a sad part about a dog."

"I just came home to change. I have to get to work."

I follow him inside. He goes upstairs, then comes

down a minute later in a new shirt, grins, and tosses me the dirty one.

I catch it, then let it drop. "Yuck!" Guy sweat.

"Can you throw that into the laundry for me? I gotta go."

"To the pool?"

"Yeah . . . that's where I work, last I checked."

My friends who went on the adventure trip are back in town, and they invited me to the pool today.

"Wait!" I head toward the stairs. "Can I go with you?"

"Sure. C'mon."

I change fast, grab a towel and sunglasses, and then hop into the front seat of the Jeep, shoving aside a mess of candy wrappers, pop cans, another smelly T-shirt.

Matt parks at the pool, then ducks behind the cashier desk and waves me in. "She's my sister," he tells a guy in a red lifeguard jacket.

The girls—Leah, Sadie, Cass, and Rachel—are already there. They've saved a spot for my towel. They hug me and say, "How's your summer?" and "We missed you," and "What's been going on?" Then Sadie tells what must be an inside joke from their trip, and Cass brings up a story about Leah getting stuck in her sleeping bag. They're laughing and calling each other nicknames, like Scout and Chico. They're all wearing black bikini bottoms with tops in different colors. My bikini is matching. Nobody told me to mix. After a while, they're still talking about the trip, so I stretch out on my stomach. Close my eyes. Zone out.

When I look up, they're in the pool, splashing each other. I'm getting burnt anyway, so I visit Matt.

"What's wrong?" he asks.

"Oh, well, they went on a trip. I didn't. Awkward."

Matt hands me a candy bar. "Have a Kit Kat."

"Shouldn't I pay?"

"Don't worry about it. Listen, going into freshman year is such a messed-up time. Everything changes."

"I know! It feels so—" A big crowd lines up behind me, and he starts ringing them up. The chocolate is melting. I finish the candy bar and lick my fingers.

"Slob," Matt says, and grins.

The girls come out with my towel, and Rachel says, "My mom can drive you home."

We don't have a lot to say on the ride. I get out. "Thanks for inviting me."

"Sure. We'll make plans."

"Okay."

Rachel's pushing buttons on the radio. "See ya."

Matt's sweaty shirt is lying on the floor where I dropped it.

I pick it up and remember doing the world's largest jigsaw puzzle with him one winter break when we had twenty inches of snow, and how we ate ice cream for dinner when Mom and Dad weren't home, and watched the first Harry Potter so many times we could recite every single line in the movie.

Curled-up leaves swirl where the Jeep was parked.

I go to the laundry room and put his shirt into a basket. Thirty-nine.

And I stand there. I could cry, but I don't.

_23_

My grandma died one year ago tomorrow. I might be the only one who remembers the date. Or if Mom, Dad, and Matt remember, they haven't said anything.

She was eighty, and something had been wrong with her heart for a while. Last spring, she decided not to have another surgery. Her body had had enough.

Mom fought her. Because Mom fights for everything. But Grandma had made up her mind. She was tired of taking pills and going to doctors and having surgeries and treatments. She was all right with it. She started saying her goodbyes. She held me close and said she would miss me terribly.

Not as much as I miss her.

She came to live with us in March, until right before the end. She was always there when I got home from school. She told me lots of STs, like she wanted to share as many as she could before she was gone.

The second time she told me I was an old soul, she said she was one too. We were sitting on the love seat on the patio. "They don't come around that often," she said. "They're an endangered species. You're very lucky. And special."

The funeral home gave us packets of forget-me-not seeds to plant in her memory. They handed them out to everyone, but people put them down when they came to our house after the funeral. Then no one remembered to take them when they left.

I collected every packet (eleven) from counters and tables and one next to a pillow on the sofa.

This is on the back of each packet:

The forget-me-not is a delicate, beautiful flower that evokes the power and memory of love. Plant them in a place that is dear to you. As they grow and bloom, your love—and your loved one—will live on.

Time for number forty.

After dinner, as dusk starts to come over the cul-de-sac, I pull a chair next to my bedroom window, hold the packets of seeds, and wait. I feel a little like Mrs. Millman, the spy of the neighborhood.

The sky deepens from blue to navy. My parents knock on my door and come in to say good night. I hear them go into their bedroom. Brush their teeth. Creaking of the floor. Their low voices as they talk. Then quiet.

Black sky now, and I wish on the first star. My clock turns 11:11, and I wish on that too.

At 11:42, I see what I've been waiting for. Mr. Dembrowski's garage door slides open. A car starts to back out. A regular four-door brown car, with an ordinary man in the driver's seat. He backs onto the street, turns, then drives away slowly.

Thomas was right.

I tiptoe down the stairs, into the garage, and grab the digging tool I used to plant the marigolds. I let myself out the front door and close it with a soft click.

It's a different place at night. The dark, silent houses are as still as mountains. A light wind circles the trees. Intoxicating, heavy summer air. The moon high and white in the sky. I walk across the grass, moist under my bare feet, then go around the side of Mr. Dembrowski's.

We should have made up for the shoe trampling. We should have done something right then.

After we ruined his garden that night, Mr. Dembrowski seemed to lose his passion for flowers. I don't think he ever planted a garden like that again. I'd see a few daisies, maybe, or some black-eyed Susans, but nothing like it was. And in the last few years, no flowers at all.

There's a light on in the back of Mr. D.'s house. I stand and look at the garden first—a small rectangle of dirt. Then I kneel and dig a narrow trench across one side. I pull one of the forget-me-not packets out of my shorts pocket. It's close enough to midnight that this is tomorrow.

I slowly sprinkle the seeds in, then cover them with dirt. "Hi, Grandma."

As I'm starting the second trench, I sense movement. A shadow. Footsteps. Animal or human? I hold up the digging tool, like it could protect me.

I jump when I hear, "Neen? What're you doing?"

And I look up at Eli.

24

He grins at me. "Lower your weapon. I come in peace."

I stand. My heart slows down. "Ha ha. You didn't have to sneak up."

"I wasn't sneaking. So, um, Neen? What are you doing?"

"I'm— Wait. What are *you* doing?"

"I asked you first."

"Okay. Well, I'm planting flower seeds."

"I was walking. Couldn't sleep." He looks at the packets. "Planting? At twelve-fifteen?"

"Yeah." I smile. It's hard not to smile at Eli. "You got a problem with that?"

"No. I guess not. But here? And now? And, okay, can I ask why?"

"Don't you remember that night we ruined Mr. D.'s flower bed?"

He scratches his cheek. "Uh . . . no."

"We ran through it, playing hide-and-seek. We were little. Me and you and Jorie. And he got mad and wanted our shoes."

"Oh, yeah." Eli laughs. "Crazy guy."

"No, he's not crazy. That's the thing. Our parents were the crazy ones. Overprotective."

"So after all these years, you just decided to come out here and fix his garden? In the middle of the night?"

"Yes. This is when he leaves his house."

"Okay . . ."

I kneel and continue digging. Eli's just standing there, watching.

"Why are you doing all these things?" he asks. "It's you, isn't it? All this stuff that's been going on?"

I keep digging.

"Neen?"

"You know the answer." I open a second packet of seeds and sprinkle them into the dirt.

Eli shoves his hands into the pockets of his shorts. "You haven't told me why, though."

I smooth dirt over the seeds and look up at him. "You really want to know?"

"Yes." He sits in the grass, stretches his legs out.

I start my third trench, then search his expression. Can I trust him? I want to. Try to explain this to someone. Maybe even to myself. But I don't know where he's at right now.

I sit back and remember how I drew the neighborhood houses on my poster board, eight separate squares that looked like they were floating in space. "You know all those movies, with heroes who fight aliens and monsters and powerful emperors and wizards gone bad . . . ridding the world of evil?"

"Yeah?"

"Well, what if that isn't it at all? I mean, what if the bad stuff isn't that obvious? It's just sort of a part of things, all around us, but we don't exactly see it. What if it's . . . *us*? Like, the way we act? Or don't act?"

"I'm sort of following you," Eli says.

"And what if the solution is just . . . good? Plain, simple, small good things, so unnoticed, so unremarkable that they're remarkable. And what if ordinary people could be the heroes?" I gesture to the dark houses. "Right here."

Eli doesn't say anything. His T-shirt ripples in the breeze.

I tear open another packet of seeds.

He moves some dirt with the toe of his shoe.

Then we look at each other, for what seems like a while, even though it's probably a few seconds.

And I have that feeling again. About a kiss.

But. He stands. "I'll get some water."

When he comes back, I've emptied six packets of forget-me-not seeds into Mr. Dembrowski's flower bed. Eli and I plant the rest together until we've filled up the entire garden. Then Eli soaks the dirt with his watering can.

"You think they'll grow?" I ask.

"I don't know."

We're just standing there. I don't want to go back inside, and I can tell Eli doesn't either. I should feel tired but I don't. The moon is smaller and higher. Farther away but right above our heads.

I sigh. "Do you ever miss when we were little?"

"Sometimes."

"My grandma died one year ago today."

Eli nods. "So that's why you wanted to do this tonight?"

"Yeah."

He looks away. "Sometimes I wish my dad was dead. Life would be a lot easier."

I gulp. "Oh, Eli, is it that bad? I'm really sorry. . . ." I want to grab his hand, but he takes a step away. "Thomas kind of told me about the money thing. . . ."

"Yeah, well, it sucks." He shoves his hair off his forehead, then gestures to the dirt. "See, my dad, he wouldn't get this. He'd never get stuff like this." Eli picks up the watering can, turns, and starts walking.

"Wait, Eli." I gather up the empty seed packets and wipe the digging tool on the grass. He has already reached my house. When I get there, he's standing on the edge of his driveway.

"I agree with you that bad stuff is right around us. I get what you're saying. But the truth is, good doesn't work for everyone," Eli says. "Some people—a lot of people—just don't understand good. They're always looking for something else. Only thinking of themselves."

I walk to him. "No. You're wrong."

"Flowers? Foot pads? You're so naive. As if those could change anything."

"You don't really believe that, do you? Like you don't have any hope?"

"It's sweet, Nina, but if you ask me, people are too messed up. This world is too messed up for little things to matter."

I narrow my eyes and take a step back. "I never asked you."

25

I didn't know Eli had gotten like that.

Jorie will be better for him. She's fun, and doesn't worry about the world. Maybe she's a new soul.

I refuse to believe what he said. Another trait of old souls—stubbornness.

41. I water the forget-me-not seeds daily. No word from Mr. D., so I don't know if he saw the dug-up dirt in the back of his house.

42. I still water Mrs. Chung's marigolds, and Mrs. Bennett's little pot. Both are blooming out of control.

43. When I find an unopened box of golf balls in

our basement (Dad tried the game—way too slow for his hyperspeed), I drop a few of them on the Millmans' lawn, and sure enough, the next day, Mr. Millman is out there practicing his swing. He hits one into the Dixon weeds, then turns and faces the other direction.

Mrs. Millman is outside too, her mahjong bag snug against her hip. A little tuft of white fur is sticking out of the top. She scans the houses, opens the bag, and peeks inside. "No sign of anything, Beanie. It's safe again." A whimper comes from inside the bag.

"Whatever it was must be gone," she tells Mr. Millman. "The smells must have driven it away."

"Myrna," he says, inspecting his golf club, "you're a little obsessed with that dog, you know."

"Don't start with me, Stan."

Mrs. Millman sits on a chair in her driveway and lifts Beanie out of the bag.

"It's all right," Mrs. Millman says, petting her. She tries to put Beanie on the ground, but the dog is clawing at Mrs. Millman's arms and yelping.

"Oh, for God's sake, bring her inside, Myrna!" Mr. Millman shouts.

She grabs Beanie and disappears into her house. Just me and the whooshing sound of Mr. Millman's golf club.

I hear "Neeenaaa!" and look over to see Thomas on the other side of the bushes between our houses.

I wave.

He separates the bushes with his hands and whispers, "I need Mystery Girl!"

"You do?"

"Yeah. Can you call her up?"

"Maybe. What's wrong?"

He pummels through the bushes, then turns around to show me the back of his cape. "Ripped again," he says sadly.

"Maybe you shouldn't keep cutting through bushes." I smile and stroke his arm.

"But that's where the bad guys hide!"

Should have known that. "Right. I'm sure I can contact Mystery Girl. You'll have to give me the cape, though, okay?"

He nods solemnly. I help him untie it, then fold the cape in my lap.

"How come it keeps breaking?" His eyes are big, full of questions.

"I don't know. But when things break, we just have to keep fixing them."

He looks small and defenseless in only his shorts and T-shirt.

"Hey, you're wearing clothes today," I say, and tickle him. He jumps away, giggling.

Then he frowns. "Eli said I have to. So when I go to kindergarten, people won't think I'm weird."

My heart breaks a little. Thomas has to start living by the rules because he's going to school. I flash ahead and see him getting off the bus with a tired face and a backpack instead of a sword. Pretty soon he'll forget all about being a hero, and the bad guys in the bushes, even though they'll still be there. He just won't see them anymore.

But it's still summer.

"Thomas," I say. "I'll get Mystery Girl to fix your cape, and I'll bring it back to you. Promise."

"Hurry, okay?" He trots back through the bushes.

Later, Mom and Dad are on the sofa, drinking coffee.

"Nina!" Dad calls. "Come see this! We were on the news today!" He holds up his phone and plays a video. Fine and Ross being interviewed by a reporter.

"Cool."

Dad turns the phone toward himself and plays it again.

Mom smiles. "How many times have you watched that, Steven?"

"I lost count. You know, I look pretty good on TV."

"We had four calls today from prospective clients," Mom tells me. "I think we're getting famous."

There's some gargantuan blond woman standing next to them in the video. "Who's that?" I ask.

Mom takes a sip of her coffee. "Melanie."

"Whoa." She's one of those women who's obviously addicted to plastic surgery. Big lips, big breasts, big hair. She could be on a reality show.

"Don't let her looks fool you. She's tough. And smart."

"Okay. . . ."

Mom's phone rings, and she stares at it. "It's like she heard us say her name." She answers. "Hi, Melanie. . . ." Mom listens, nodding. "No problem. Yes. Don't worry. We'll take care of it. Get a good night's sleep, all right? We'll talk in the morning."

Mom hangs up, shakes her head. "Now I'm her therapist too."

I raise my eyebrows. "Grandma would have said, 'That woman needs a good talking-to.' "

Mom looks pained. "I suppose she would have."

Awkward silence.

Dad stands, picks up the coffee cups. "Everything okay, my girl?"

"Yeah." I shrug. "My phone's having issues, though. In case you try to call me and it doesn't go through."

He goes into the kitchen, rinses the cups. "Nina. What is it with you and phones?"

Just Mom and me on the sofa. She's staring off into space.

I bite my lip. "I didn't mean to make you sad."

"I'm not sad." She pats my knee, then gets up abruptly and goes upstairs.

In the middle of the night, I wake and hear a noise. I creep halfway down the stairs and see Mom sitting at the kitchen table, with an open shoe box. Crying. There are all sorts of papers and index cards, and she's shuffling through them, like she's looking for something.

I know that shoe box.

It was Grandma's.

26

The next morning, I don't see the box, and I sneak Grandma's sewing basket up to my room so Mom won't get upset. Does mending Thomas's cape again count as another good thing? So what? This is forty-four.

The last time Mom and Grandma were together, they had a fight. Maybe that was the only way they could end, after a lifetime of arguing. Mom was pleading with Grandma to take her medicines and have the surgery so she could get more time. Grandma kept saying, "For what?"

"You are the most difficult woman I've ever known," Mom said.

Grandma's hands were in her lap. "As are you."

Both were right.

Mom was at work on the day Grandma actually died. I wasn't with Grandma either. She was in hospice then, in a bed all the time. One of the nurses, Shelley, told us she thought Grandma had waited to die when she was alone. "It's a strange thing," Shelley said. "I've seen it happen again and again. People wait until their loved ones aren't in the room. They somehow know."

That night, I'm in my room, about to thread the needle, when I see a flash of light from the Dixon house. *What* is going on?

I put Thomas's cape down, then go outside and make my way across the empty, dark street, walking around the circle of grass in the middle, watching for anything—an animal, the *kumiho,* Eli, stray bad guys. Everything feels spooky tonight, and goose bumps trickle across my arms. The way the wind skirts through the lawns. The moon partly covered by a cloud. Tree branches scraping against a house. Maybe I should have worn the cape. I don't doubt its protective powers.

I walk slowly along the Millmans' grass toward the back of the Dixon house. The house is dark and silent, but there's a bad smell, like spoiled milk. And mothballs. I hear an engine revving in the distance. A screech of tires. The pop of a firecracker.

The weeds are wet and sticky around my legs; then my foot kicks something. A glass bottle shoots a few feet ahead of me. A strip of moonlight shows more. There must be at least ten dark bottles, most under a dead pine tree. Plus crumpled chip bags, candy wrappers, and apple cores. Like some kids had a party back here.

I look down the street that leads out of the cul-de-sac. No cars. Whoever was here is gone. They must have parked somewhere else. I pick up one of the bottles. Hard to tell what it is in the dark. No label.

A mosquito buzzes near my face, and I wave it away. I can't just leave all this. It's completely gross. Flies are circling the apple cores. I walk back to my house and get a garbage bag, then quickly clean up. Number forty-five, I suppose. Although why does this one feel different? It makes me think about what Eli said—the world is messed up and some people just don't care.

I knot the bag, pick it up, and turn the corner around the back of the house.

A voice shouts from the darkness. "Aha! Caught ya!"

Mrs. Millman is standing in her bathrobe, pointing a flashlight into my eyes.

27

Is she insane?

"What's in the bag?" She laughs crazily.

I come up with something brilliant: "Um . . ."

"Well?" Mrs. Millman moves the flashlight over the bag. Her hand is shaking.

She has her hair in some sort of net thing, and there's whitish cream around her eyes. She's scarier than any tree or fox. Maybe the *kumiho* has already shape-shifted into an evil woman and it has been Mrs. Millman all along. Did Mrs. Chung ever think of that?

"I saw a light," I say.

She takes a step closer to me. "And? What was it?"

"I just found some garbage." I gesture to the Dixon house. "Back there."

Mrs. Millman crosses her arms. "What kind of garbage?"

What is she, a detective? "Like, bottles, candy wrappers. You know, *garbage*."

"Bottles? Was it alcohol?"

"I don't know."

I think she's going to grab the bag, open it, and inspect the contents, but she says, "Did you see anyone?"

I shake my head. "No."

She takes a few more steps until she's standing just inches from my face. She's scarier up close. If that's even possible.

"There is something going on. That *house*. A wild animal attacks an innocent dog. Now it sounds like a group of reckless kids are using it as their hangout." She lowers her voice. "I suspect paranormal activity as well."

I stare at her.

"I watch that TV show. The signs are all there."

"Wait. You mean, like, ghosts?"

"Exactly!"

Mrs. Chung is convinced there's a nine-tailed fox spirit stalking the neighborhood; now Mrs. Millman suspects ghosts. Okay.

She adjusts her net thing, and I shift the bag to my other hand. Who would believe this? I am standing in the Dixon weeds in the middle of the night, holding a bag of gross garbage, talking with Mrs. Millman about ghosts.

"What kind of signs?" I ask.

"Lights, noises, shadows, faces in the window. This place is haunted!"

"You've seen faces in the window?" Creepy. If true. Doubtful.

She clicks off the flashlight and nods briskly. "Yes, I have, and I suppose it's up to me to do something. Like always." She gathers her bathrobe closer. "I'm watching you," she says, doing that thing with her fingers in a V, first toward her eyes, then toward me. "I'm watching everyone."

She stomps back to her house.

I walk home and cram the bag into our garbage can.

I'm watching too.

The next morning, there's a huge sign on Eli's garage for the entire neighborhood to see.

E + J = HC.

Oh, God.

There it is. They're going to homecoming.

Matt is leaning against his Jeep, eating a bowl of cereal. He looks like he slept in his shirt. "Who's J?"

"Jorie."

"I didn't know they were going out."

"It's just a thing right now. Last I heard."

"I always thought Eli had a thing for you."

"Apparently not." But then I say, "Why'd you think that?" I'm blushing.

Matt shrugs. "Guys can tell."

"Well, it's not true."

"Weird, though. The guy asks to homecoming." Matt gestures to the sign with his spoon. "The girl asks to Turnabout. So why would the sign be on Eli's garage? Is Jorie asking him?"

I don't know, but I have this urge to run over and rip that sign off.

Matt looks at me. "You okay?"

"Why wouldn't I be okay? Of course I'm okay. Don't I look okay?"

"Just asking." He spills the milk out into the grass. "I gotta go." He hands me the bowl. "Bring this in for me?"

I hand it back to him. "I'm not your servant."

He raises his eyebrows.

"What?" I snap.

"Hey, if you're mad about that"—he points to the sign—"don't take it out on me."

"Yeah, why would you want to get involved? Why would you care?"

"Huh?"

"Just go, Matt. Like always. Things get bad, you take off. Close up."

He's staring at me. "What does that mean?"

I see Jorie's mom backing out of their driveway. "I don't know. Think about it. I'm leaving."

Matt says, "Hey!" but I start walking.

When I get into the backseat, Jorie lets out a sigh. Then another, and another. She's just waiting for me to ask.

I finally give in. "So you and Eli are going to home-coming?"

"Yes," she breathes.

I have to say it. "He asked you?"

"More or less."

I feel sick.

"I'm happy for you. You guys are good for each other. Did you get the red dress?"

"I still can't decide. But I have time." She turns to me. "I want you to go in the group with me and Eli. So I've made a list of potential dates."

"Seriously?"

She's completely serious. "So far I've come up with three." She shows me the list on her phone: Leo Berman, Raj Patel, and Grady Brunson.

First, I don't know any of these boys, except for a face in the hall. Second, I don't want Jorie to choose a date for me. Third, I don't even know what third is. And fourth, this is not how you dream about these events in your life.

"Isn't Leo Berman shorter than me?" I ask.

"So you won't wear heels."

"And I thought Raj had a girlfriend."

"They broke up."

"Oh."

"Listen, Nina, tell me you'll think about it. Because it will be such a fun night, and I really want you to be there. We'll get our hair and nails done and get ready together." She makes these puppy-dog eyes. "It's the beginning of everything! Our whole high school lives! Say okay! Okay?"

"But . . . I don't really know Leo or Raj or Grady. Why would they even ask me?"

We're at school. Jorie opens the car door. "Not a problem."

"Jorie! Wait!" I call, but she's off. She's probably going to find one of those boys right now. I have the urge to reel her in with a very scratchy rope.

"Thanks for driving us," I say to her mom.

"Nina?" She's looking back at me. I realize she didn't give us one of her warnings.

"Yeah?"

"Watch out for her, would you?"

I nod. "I'll try."

She slides off her sunglasses. She looks sort of sad. "Thank you, honey."

Forty-six.

In art, Ms. Quinlan is showing our perspective drawings and commenting on each. When she holds up mine, she says, "Interesting viewpoint. I like how you've drawn the circle of houses. Where were you standing?"

"I was sitting in a hammock."

Chase nods. Sariah tips her head to the side.

Ms. Quinlan hands it back to me. "What's that, at the last house?"

"It's a fox."

"Nice touch. Adds a little mystery."

Thomas is waiting for me when I get home. The cape. After cleaning up the mysterious garbage and having my nighttime heart-to-heart with Myrna Millman, I forgot to sew his cape.

"Thomas," I say.

He has his arms crossed. "I need my cape fixed. Today! The bad guys are getting closer!"

"I know. I'm really sorry. I got a little busy. I mean—"

"What do you mean, *you* got busy?" Thomas's eyes get wide. "Wait, are you . . . Mystery Girl?"

"No, no, I'm not, but I know her very well."

"You're really not her?"

"Um, yeah." Mr. D. and Eli already know; Thomas will tell everyone else, and who knows what Mrs. Millman will do then. Turn me over to the authorities, I suppose, although what would they charge me with? Premeditated good?

"Well, could you tell her I really, really, really need my cape back?"

"Yes, sir." I salute him.

He trots back into his house. The homecoming sign has been taken down.

I see a piece of paper taped to our front door: URGENT

(all caps, red ink). Mrs. Millman has called another meeting.

> *Please meet in the center of our cul-de-sac this evening at 8 p.m. to discuss the peculiar goings-on in our neighborhood. We can no longer ignore this vitally important matter.*
>
> *Mrs. Myrna Millman*

I doubt my parents will go. I leave the note on the kitchen table, then run upstairs, grab Thomas's cape, and spread it across my lap. I remove the button tray from the sewing basket and dig for the black thread, but a long piece is caught around two other spools. When I pull everything out to untangle them, somehow, *somehow,* Grandma's wedding band falls into my palm. The one that was lost. A thin band with tiny chips of diamonds. From her fifty-two-year marriage to my grandpa. She wanted to be buried with it, but no one could find it. No one thought to look in her sewing basket. And here it is.

There is nothing else to do but slip it onto my finger.

I twist the band around and wish I could somehow get it to her. A good thing that I will never be able to do.

At the funeral, I couldn't stand up in front of everyone and share memories of her. Mom spoke, Mom's sister spoke, and one of my cousins. They all talked about how she loved her family, and tradition, and of course, things like sewing and cooking and holidays, and how she just simply couldn't understand email. Mom joked about her too, which is something I guess people do at funerals.

But none of them really got her.

At first I felt sad that I wasn't able to get up and talk. But then I thought she'd have been okay with it. Because we got each other. And we both knew it. So why did I need to tell everyone else?

I take off the band and hold it up to my window, sunlight catching in the tiny diamonds. Maybe Grandma wasn't meant to be buried with her wedding band. Maybe it was meant for me. From one old soul to another. What if, this whole year, it was waiting for me at the bottom of her sewing basket? A treasure in the most unlikely place. Or the most likely place, really, when you think about it. And I found it because of a good thing I'm doing—sewing Thomas's cape.

With her band back on my finger, I thread the needle and sew the ripped part of the cape. Small, even stitches. Then I bring it to Thomas's house. Except Eli answers the door.

"Oh. Um. Is your brother here?" I ask.

"He fell asleep." Eli reaches for the cape. "Here, I'll take it."

"Okay." I turn.

"Wait, Nina?"

"What?" My "what" is sharper than I meant it to come out, and I don't know why. Yeah, I do. That *sign*.

"Just, thanks for fixing it again."

"Sure."

We glance at each other; then he twists his mouth a little, looks away.

"Well," I say. He's gone over to Jorie Land. I start to walk away, then turn back as he's closing the door. I touch Grandma's band. "Eli. This little thing? Fixing the cape? To Thomas, it's huge. Can't you see that?"

"I mean, yeah, but it doesn't make a difference in the real world." He balls up the fabric in his hand. "It's pretend."

I shake my head. "Not to me, or Thomas."

"Whatever."

He shuts the door.

30

I have never seen so many people on the street at one time. Mrs. Chung on her crutches. Mrs. Cantaloni, with her arms around her stomach. Her three boys and Thomas, wrestling on the Cantalonis' front lawn. Jorie's mom and dad. Mr. Millman, a cigar tucked into his shirt pocket. Mrs. Bennett in her nursing scrubs.

And, unbelievable. Fine and Ross. They've left the kitchen table.

I'm taking it all in from my favorite spot—the hammock. A perfect view.

Mrs. Millman is ecstatic. "Thank you all for

coming." She clasps her hands. "I believe we are facing a crisis here, and it is of vital importance that we discuss how to handle this situation."

"Yes, Myrna, we received your note," Dad says sarcastically.

"As most of you know, my poodle, Beanie, was the victim of an attack by an animal in those weeds." Mrs. Millman waves her hand at the Dixon house. "She is suffering from post-traumatic stress syndrome."

Jorie's dad laughs. "I didn't know a dog could get that."

"This is not funny!" Mrs. Millman snaps.

"Sorry. My sincere apologies."

"Secondly, it has come to my attention that someone is using the vacant Dixon property as a hangout. My guess is teenagers. Most likely drinking."

The neighbors look distressed. "That's not good," Mrs. Cantaloni says.

Mrs. Millman nods. "I have asked the police to patrol the area more frequently."

Jorie's mom pats her arm. "Good idea."

"Thanks for taking the lead on that," Jorie's dad says. "Has anyone seen the kids? Know who they are?"

"No," Mrs. Millman reports. "But believe me, I will stay on it."

I'm surprised she hasn't said anything about me and

that night. Probably wants to take all the credit for being on top of things.

My parents have been quiet. They're checking their phones.

"However, neither of these incidents is our biggest problem anymore," Mrs. Millman says.

Mrs. Bennett yawns. "Oh, excuse me. Long shift."

"What's our biggest problem?" Jorie's mom asks.

Mrs. Millman lowers her voice, and I have to lean forward. "I now believe that everything that's been happening around here all summer . . . is the work of otherworldly spirits."

"You mean ghosts?" Mrs. Cantaloni asks.

"Yes."

"Oh, come on!" That's Dad. "You didn't call us out here to tell us you think ghosts are haunting that house? I don't believe in that stuff."

"Agree," Mom echoes.

"Well, let's listen to her point of view," Mrs. Bennett says. "Go on, Myrna. Why do you think that?"

Mrs. Millman describes the lights, noises, shadows, and faces she's seen. "And haven't you all noticed the highly unusual goings-on? Pennies in people's mailboxes? Golf balls and cigars popping up out of nowhere? A smiley face balloon in my flowerpot?"

Dad is staring at Mrs. Millman. "Maybe you should talk to someone, Myrna. Someone professional."

"I'm not crazy!"

Mrs. Chung has been quiet until now. "It's the *kumiho*."

Dad turns to her. "Excuse me?"

"Fox spirit."

Everyone stares at her for a minute; then they start talking at the same time. I can't make sense of anything.

Then Dad shouts, "Stop, everyone! Settle down!" He turns to Mrs. Millman. "Look, Myrna, while there may be some issues with the Dixon house, you've already notified the police, so I'm not sure what else we can do at this point. As for what you're calling 'unusual things,' I just don't see anything there. It all sounds harmless. I'm sure everything has a reasonable explanation. Coincidence. And ghosts?" He looks around at the other neighbors. "I don't think you have a lot of support for your argument."

Mrs. Millman starts to say something, but the meeting breaks up.

"We should get together," Jorie's mom says to mine. "It's been so long since we had dinner."

"It has." Mom nods. "We've been immersed in this case. The summer is just speeding by. I still have to buy everything Matt needs for college."

"College! Hard to believe. Where did the time go?"

"I know," Mom says, and for a second, she looks . . .

different. Softer? Her face. Her shoulders. Something . . . I think of that night, when I saw her crying.

"I'll email you some dates," Jorie's mom says.

"Email?" Mrs. Chung laughs. "Why? Talk."

Dad and Jorie's dad shake hands. Mrs. Bennett asks
Mrs. Cantaloni how she's feeling. The Cantaloni boys
and Thomas start a game of monkey in the middle.
Mrs. Chung claps when Jordan catches the ball. "Good
for you!" she calls.

Unusual things indeed.

This is a huge number forty-seven.

I'm counting it even though I didn't do anything.

Or did I?

Jorie is having people over and invites me.

She didn't mention that "people" include the three boys she decided are my potential homecoming dates.

She didn't say anything about boys at all, so I'm wearing an old pair of jean shorts and a T-shirt of Matt's that shrank in the wash. And my glasses. Not the greatest first impression. If I wanted to make one.

There are a bunch of people from her class too. And Eli's friends Tyler and Sam, who are calling Jorie "chocolate girl." But I don't see Eli.

I spot the boys:

1. Leo Berman hasn't grown since about sixth grade. He's nice, but I just can't get past the height issue. He barely reaches my nose.

2. Raj Patel has had about ten girlfriends, each lasting two weeks. Do I want to be number eleven? Besides, Raj seems like the kind of guy who would take off and find someone else during the dance.

3. I realize that Grady Brunson is the guy in the plaid shorts who always throws around Jorie's water bottle. He wouldn't go to homecoming with me in a million years. I don't know what Jorie was even thinking.

But the weirdest thing of all is that Sariah is here. I have to say hi. If I don't, we'll be eyeing each other all night and it'll just be more awkward than ever.

So I do. (Forty-eight.)

"You know Jorie?" I ask her.

"Not really. I'm friends with Raj."

Was she one of his girlfriends?

We avoid each other's eyes for a second. Then I say, "Want to sit somewhere?"

She shrugs. "Okay."

Jorie turns up the music, and Sariah and I find a spot on the floor.

I pull a thread on my shorts. "How's your self-portrait going?" Our final project in art.

"Oh. Good. Yours?"

I smile. "I'm having some problems with my eyes. Drawing them, I mean."

"I can help you."

"That would be good. They don't look human."

She laughs.

"So . . . anything you want to tell me about frogs?"

"Oh my God." She covers her face for a second. "I am so weird sometimes! I really do have a frog collection, but when I get nervous, I start saying all these odd, random thoughts. They just pop out, like I can't help myself. You must think I'm so strange."

Wait. Random thoughts?

Turns out, Sariah has a whole brain full of odd things to say, only they don't seem so strange anymore. She's funny and quick, and keeps making hilarious observations about people at the party. I can't stop laughing.

We're about to get some pizza, but Jorie is dragging Grady Brunson over. "Why are you hiding in the corner?" she says to me. Then to Sariah, "Oh, hi."

I stand. Immediate this-is-so-wrong feeling. Definitely mutual, as Grady looks at the wall to the right of my face.

"Grades," Jorie sings, "this is Neeennna."

"Hi." He looks at some girls at the other end of the room.

He's very cute, if you like guys with long stringy hair, low-hanging baggy jeans, leather flip-flops, a wrinkled Hollister T-shirt. Guys who are rude to girls like me.

"So," Jorie says loudly, "I was just telling Grades that you are thinking of going out for girls' basketball."

I am?

"Grades plays basketball," Jorie says, threading her arm through his. "And he's really good. He'll probably make varsity. Isn't that amazing?"

Well, it's a match. We have tons to talk about.

"I played one year in junior high," I say. "Point guard. I didn't start, though. I'm not sure I'm good enough for a high school team. I'm only five-one."

Why am I talking? Grady's not even listening, and Jorie has drifted off. Sariah stands. "I played in junior high too."

"Really?"

"Also point guard."

Grady shifts his feet. Sariah rolls her eyes.

"It's okay," I tell him. "You don't have to stay and talk to us."

He tips his head at me, the first acknowledgment that I'm here. "See ya around, Gina."

I make a face as he walks away.

Sariah says, "Jerk."

"Yeah, my grandma would have said that boy hasn't got a lot upstairs."

"So true."

Jorie marches over. "What happened?" she whispers. "I set the whole thing up. I bragged about your basketball skills for, like, twenty minutes. Told him you were sweet and funny and, like, a really helpful person."

"Forget it," I say, my voice low.

"Oh God, Nina, you're hopeless." Jorie's still whispering. Sariah has moved away a little.

"Thanks. Thanks a lot. He couldn't even remember my name."

"I'm just saying. You have to make it happen, you know?"

I narrow my eyes. "I'm fine, okay?"

Jorie does that half-smile-raised-lips thing. "Whatevs."

Sariah and I talk the rest of the night. Finish each other's sentences. A hundred random thoughts. But nothing about frogs.

When I'm home and fall into bed, I smile at the ceiling. Is it possible I found someone who gets me?

32

It takes Mom a few days to notice that I've been wearing Grandma's band.

She's at the kitchen sink, rinsing carryout containers, and I'm sitting at the counter, finishing my self-portrait. My eyes look a lot better since Sariah gave me some tips.

Mom turns off the water. "Is that my mother's ring?"

I nod. "I found it in her sewing basket."

She dries her hands and sits across from me. "Really."

I slip it off and give it to her. Mom holds it in her

palm. "Her sewing basket." She shakes her head. "Of course. Why didn't anyone think of that? Why didn't we look there?"

She puts it on her finger, but it goes only about half-way. "She had such small hands." Mom gives it back to me, nods. "You have her hands. Every time I see your hands, I see hers."

I slip the band back on.

"It fits you perfectly."

We're quiet. The wall clock ticks. Dad is snoring on the sofa in the family room. All their papers are put away.

Mom swallows. "It's been a year."

"Last week."

She hesitates, then reaches her hand across the counter and covers mine. "You miss her?"

"I do. So much." I blink back tears.

"I keep thinking about those dinners at her apartment, how she'd annoy me, but now . . . I don't even remember what it was that upset me. . . . I miss her too."

I twist the band.

"I thought having her stay here, when she was sick, might make things better between us. But they got worse. It was hard . . . I tried . . . I really did."

"I know."

She bites her lip. "The other night, I looked for the

162

carrot ring recipe. . . . I had a taste for it too. Went through every single one in that old shoe box."

"Did you find it?"

She shakes her head, sighs. "No. . . . What are you drawing?"

I hold up the paper. "Myself."

She takes the sketch, examines it. "Pretty good. You want to do something with art?"

"You mean for a career?"

Mom nods.

"Probably not."

"You know what you want to do?"

I grin. "Not a clue."

She smiles. "That's all right."

"Did you know—I mean, when you were thirteen?"

"I don't remember. I just didn't want . . . to be like my mother." She gets up. Pushes in the stool, goes back to the sink. Mom didn't cry when Grandma died. But her eyes are teary now.

Is this forty-nine?

I watch her squirt soap around the sink, then rinse it, sloshing the water with her hands.

She turns. "I'm glad you two were close. And that she had a granddaughter like you."

I scoot myself up onto the counter next to the sink.

"What?" she asks.

"She was proud of you. She told me."

Mom nods, wipes her eyes with the back of her hand.

She turns off the water, and we each let out a long breath.

Yes, forty-nine.

33

The next day, I'm in my room, trying to make sense of *The Alchemist,* when I hear shouting outside. Eli's arguing with a man in his driveway. His dad. I haven't seen him in a long time. An old, rusty car is parked in front of the house, with blackish exhaust coming out the back.

I run out. Eli's dad is wearing a grimy flannel shirt, jeans, and a Chicago Bears cap. He's got a stubbly beard.

"Just leave!" Eli yells. "Don't come back! Ever! We don't need you!"

"What about twenty bucks for your old man?"

Eli's cheeks are bright red. "I hate you!"

His dad picks up a basketball from the grass and heaves it into the street.

Thomas runs out of the garage to chase the ball. "Go back inside!" Eli shouts.

Eli's dad starts to throw a punch, but Eli grabs his arm. Eli is a few inches taller. They sort of push each other. Then Mrs. Bennett comes out and tries to break it up.

I'm shaking. Should I call the police? Should I get another neighbor? I'm about to run in and get my phone, but Mrs. Bennett says, calm and strong: "We're done. Get off my property. Now."

Eli half drags his dad to the car, opens the door, and shoves him inside. His dad guns the motor and speeds off. Leaves a fog of black smoke in the air.

Mrs. Bennett tries to hug Eli, but he storms away. "No!"

He clenches his hands into fists, then jumps up, hits the basketball net. Kicks the pole. He sees me and runs over. He looks a little crazy. Like he's either going to cry or explode.

"Nina!" He grabs my hand. Pulls. And starts running.

Doesn't say another word as he tears out of our neighborhood, moving fast, holding on. I'm doing all I can to keep up. We pass the park and cut through some backyards. A dog starts barking. Some kids are running through a sprinkler. Everything's a blur. I feel a cramp in my side. A woman in her car honks at us.

He doesn't let go of my hand.

Finally, Eli stops and I almost crash into him. We're at the edge of the big open field by our old elementary school. It's deserted. I bend over, hands on my knees, trying to catch my breath, trying to stop shaking.

"Have you thought about going out for cross-country?" I pant.

Eli picks up a small rock and throws it into the field. "He comes here every few months and busts into the house and looks for money. He's supposed to be giving my mom child support, right? Well, not only does that not happen, but he thinks he can just help himself to whatever cash Mom has left for me and Thomas while she's at work. I've been cutting people's lawns all summer, trying to help. The guy hasn't had a job in years."

"You stood up to him," I say softly.

"Yeah. I've done it before. He'll be back. And I'll do it again."

"Can't you get a court order to make him stay away from you?" I've heard my parents talk about that.

"We have one. I'm supposed to call the cops every time he shows up? Great life for Thomas. I hate it when

Thomas sees the fighting, but I can't help it. My dad makes me so mad." Eli walks into the field and stands there, looking out, his back to me.

The school is closed tight for the summer. No art projects hanging in the windows or from the ceilings. It feels so long ago that Eli, Jorie, and I were here. Played games at recess and learned long division and sang in concerts.

I stand next to him.

"So, see," he says. "Not everyone's good, and good things can't fix people like that."

"Maybe."

"Try giving my dad some flowers. He'd sell them. See if he could make a few bucks."

I touch his arm. "But do you think there are more people in the world like your dad, or more people like me? And you?"

He sighs, kicks at the grass. "I don't know. How can someone know that?"

"It's not if you know; it's what you hope. You can't give up, not try."

This has to be a good thing. So this is number fifty. They are getting bigger and more serious. I'm not sure if I meant that to happen.

He looks at my bare feet. "You're not wearing shoes."

"My flip-flops fell off somewhere during our marathon run."

Before I can protest, he picks me up. "What are you doing?"

"There's some broken glass." He sets me on a bench. We look at each other.

My heart is about to burst. A breeze ruffles his hair. The sun is right overhead.

"Doesn't anything not make sense to you?" he asks. "Don't you ever get so mad, you want to—"

"All the time." I smile at him.

Eli leans down, close to my face.

"Wait," I whisper. "Aren't you and . . ."

He kisses me.

34

Oh. Help. Wow.

My first kiss.

Soft and sweet and I've forgotten to take a breath.

Eli leans back and looks at me. "Neen . . ."

I've forgotten how to talk too. "Yes?"

He steps back, sticks his hands into his pockets, doesn't say anything for a few seconds. Then: "We should go. . . . I ran out so fast . . . I need to see if my mom's okay."

We walk home, both quiet. I don't see my flip-flops anywhere. Eli's walking a little ahead of me. Awkward, not sure what to say? Or impatient because I'm taking slow, careful steps in my bare feet? I can't tell.

When we get there, his mom is sitting on the grass, holding Thomas. Eli turns. "See you later, okay? Thanks. . . ."

They walk into their house and I go to my yard and lie in the hammock. I don't know what to think now.

It was only the moment. Had to be. He was upset about his dad and I happened to be there.

Right?

He's going to homecoming with Jorie. It's all set. The sign. The red dress. They have a thing. It's been going on all summer. Kissing me is not part of the thing. She would hate me forever if she found out.

It was the moment . . . *right?*

Now what?

This is complicated.

Especially because . . . I want to kiss him again.

Definitely.

Soon.

35

The next morning, I'm waiting for Jorie and her mom to drive us to the last day of summer school. I feel like she's going to know immediately, that the kiss will show on my face somehow.

No one else is outside. I'm early, so I take my daily walk over to Mr. Dembrowski's flower bed. A dozen little green sprouts are poking through the dirt. The forget-me-nots! They look fragile, and I want to protect them. Make sure they survive. It's like I've become the neighborhood flower guardian.

I hear Jorie's mom honk, and I run to their car.

I get in. "Hi."

"Raj is out," Jorie says. "He asked someone else."

"Okay. I wasn't thinking he would ask me."

"What about Grady? What did you *really* think of him?"

"Jor, you know that is not going to happen. Grady and I are on different planets."

She twirls a piece of hair. "That is not true. He thought you were cute."

"Yeah, right. At what point did he say that? Because he didn't even look at me."

"You're being so difficult, Nina. We'll have to go with Leo."

I cross my arms. "Look, I appreciate your worrying about getting me a date, but we are not going with Leo. We are not going with anyone."

Jorie's mom smiles at me in the rearview mirror as she pulls over to the curb to drop us off.

Jorie gets out and hoists her tote bag onto her shoulder. "Bye, Mom. Love you." She turns to me. "Nina, it's either Leo or Mark Oberton."

"Who's Mark Oberton?"

"He's in my class."

"No. Stop this. Please. If I want to find someone, I will."

This time I walk off, leaving Jorie behind.

I don't even look back to see how she's taking it.

Our self-portraits are hung around the room, and we're supposed to guess who's who. Some are really strange and jumbled, like a Picasso, and others, like Sariah's, are amazing. Mine? I definitely conquered the eye issue. Not Picasso, not amazing. My face. A pretty good face.

Amber is looking at my self-portrait, then at me. She nods. "You taking advanced art this year?"

"No. Are you?"

"Yeah. That one's mine." She points. "I went with abstract."

"It's good. Different."

"Thanks."

Chase comes over, sits on a desk, offers me a piece of gum.

"You're not wearing all black," I say.

He laughs, looks down at his gray T-shirt with a band's logo. "Only color they had at the concert."

Amber gently punches my shoulder. "You should take advanced. You got a lot better."

"Thanks. Maybe I will."

"Yeah, girl," Amber says.

Chase nods.

Ms. Quinlan asks me and Sariah to put up posters around the school for an art show this fall.

"It was fun the other night," Sariah says, holding a poster on the bulletin board as I push in a tack.

"It was. You're hilarious."

We head down the hall, and I tack up a second one.

"What are your classes this year?" Sariah asks.

"Accelerated English, algebra, world history, Spanish two, biology."

"When do you have lunch?"

"Fifth."

She grabs my arm. "Wait, me too!"

"That's great!"

We put up a few more posters, then get lost. The building's huge. Sariah and I finally find the commons, share a cookie, and make plans to hang out. Sariah's saying she heard they have smoothies during school, when I see Leo Berman looking at me.

"Oh God," I whisper, turning the other way.

"What?"

"Jorie's plan," I mutter. "She thinks I should go to homecoming with that guy over there."

Sariah glances in Leo's direction. "The one with the brown shirt?"

"Yeah."

"Why is she—"

"Don't even ask. I told her not to do this, but you can't stop Jorie when she gets an idea. One time, she wanted us to . . ."

I get a little catch in my throat.

I start thinking about this time when Jorie heard a

movie was being filmed downtown and she wanted us to go down there and try to be extras. Her mom said no, and mine was at work, but Jorie didn't let up until her mom finally took us. But we were too far back in line to be picked.

When we got home, she took her parents' video camera and insisted we make our own movie. We dressed up, ran around doing silly things. She called it *This Movie Is Better*. I still have the tape somewhere.

"What?" Sariah says.

"Oh, nothing."

I don't want to share it; the memory belongs to me and Jorie.

There was a lot of good between us.

I'm shooting baskets later, to burn off energy and not think. About *anything*.

Mr. and Mrs. Millman are in their driveway, talking loudly to each other on cell phones. Beanie is whimpering under a lawn chair.

"What kind of phones are these?" Mrs. Millman shouts. "Where did you buy them? Some crappy discount store?"

"From my cousin," Mr. Millman says.

"The one who runs the pawnshop?"

"So? He has very good merchandise."

"They're terrible. Don't you hear all that static? You have to return them."

"Final sale."

Mrs. Millman stamps her foot. "Final sale?" Beanie lets out a yelp. "See? She can't stand the noise either."

"Dogs are more sensitive to high frequency sounds, Myrna," Mr. Millman says. "You know that."

She tosses the phone onto the chair and reaches for Beanie. Mr. Millman groans, takes a cigar from his pocket, and sniffs it.

I'm curious. (1) What's with the new phones? And (2) Why are they married to each other?

A delivery truck drives up and stops in front of their house. The driver gets out, places a box in front of Mrs. M., and has her sign for it.

When he pulls away, Mr. Millman looks at the box. "Have you lost your mind?"

I pretend like I'm raising my hand. Yes!

"Where on earth did you get *that*?" he says.

She lifts the box. "I ordered it from a website."

He snorts. "You paid money for this? And you're complaining about the phones?"

She tips her head toward the Dixon house. "I plan to find out what is going on in that place once and for all." She turns, and I see huge letters stamped on the side of the box: TRACK A GHOST—IN FIVE EASY STEPS.

Mr. Millman says exactly what I'm thinking.

"You've got to be kidding me. Myrna, you can't just go in there—"

"Oh yes I can. Turns out, my mahjong friend's house was sold by this same realtor. He gave me the okay to check it out. He said the last thing he wants on his hands is a haunted house." Mrs. Millman carries the box inside.

Mr. Millman throws his arms into the air, like, *What am I supposed to do with her?* Then he runs after her, calling, "This I've got to see. Don't open it without me!"

Eli rings my doorbell, and when I open the door, he says, "I am in serious need of some pasta assistance."

I blush. His hair's messy and his shirt has a wet spot on the front. "What are you talking about?"

"Please tell me you know something about making pasta."

Pasta? All I can think about is the kiss. Isn't he thinking about it too?

"Um . . . sure."

He runs a hand through his hair. "Thomas and I got

this idea we'd make a real dinner, not something frozen. We're having some . . . issues."

I laugh and come outside. "Don't tell me you've decided to leave the dark side and do something good?"

He groans. "We're just trying to make dinner. Help. Please. Now."

I walk with Eli, thinking, *This is number fifty-one.*

"Neen," he says, "why are you never wearing shoes? Don't girls have, like, a hundred pairs of shoes?"

I smile. "It's summer."

He's not mentioning what happened, but it's right there. I feel it. Does he?

Inside the house, Thomas comes running, cape flying. "Mystery Girl!" he shouts.

I grab him and swing him around. "I'm not Mystery Girl."

He whispers into my ear. "I figured it out. You keep it a secret, just like all the other superheroes."

I set him down. "So what's up with the pasta?" Their house looks the same as I remember it. A worn sofa with lots of pillows. Curtains. An old TV.

"Eli made a mess!" Thomas says.

There are broken pieces of uncooked spaghetti all over the stove. "Nice." I sweep them into a pile.

Thomas climbs onto a stool.

"The pot is too small. And you know you're

supposed to boil the water before you put the noodles in?" I glance at Eli. "There is something called a cook-book. And the recipe is on the box."

He softly punches my arm.

"Do you have a bigger pot?"

He opens a cabinet and hands me one. I fill it with water and turn on the burner, add some salt.

Eli looks at all the broken noodles. "Should I open another box?"

"It's fine; they'll still taste the same."

He shakes his head and gets another box. "I want the dinner to be good, not . . . a mess."

"Do you have another pot for the sauce?"

Thomas stands on the stool. "In there!" He points his sword, and the stool starts to wobble. "Whoa!"

Eli runs and grabs him before he falls. "Sit on the stool, Tom." Eli plunks him down.

Thomas frowns and crosses his arms. "What kind of superhero has to sit down?"

Eli's phone buzzes, and he pulls it out of his pocket, then texts someone.

I pour the sauce into the pot. The spaghetti water starts boiling.

"Thanks," Eli says, coming over to look. "Much better."

"Put in the spaghetti."

He does, and I hand him a spoon. "Stir. So it doesn't stick."

"Okay."

"Can I sing you a song?" Thomas asks me.

"Sure."

"I made it up."

"All right."

"Don't be afraid! Don't be scared! Thomas Bennett is here! And he can fight a bear!"

He grins, and I clap. "That was great!"

Eli smiles, still stirring.

I glance around. "What else are you making? Garlic bread? Salad?"

Thomas and Eli look at each other. Eli says, "I guess."

The door to their garage flies opens. Jorie calls, "E?"

E?

She walks in. "What's going on? You guys are cooking?" She takes the spoon from Eli. "I make amazing spaghetti."

Since when?

"Eli's cooking it," Thomas tells her.

Jorie adjusts the burner. "Now, you want them al dente, not mushy."

Who is she?

"Oh." Eli watches her.

Jorie picks a noodle up with the spoon and holds it to Eli's mouth. "See if it's done."

He chews, shrugs. "I think so."

"Perfect," Jorie says. "Where's that strainer thing?"

I want to throw the boiling pot at someone. I'm not sure who.

Eli turns off the burner. "Thomas, where's the . . ."

"It's called a colander," I say.

"That bowl with the little holes? There." Thomas points.

Eli takes out the colander, puts it in the sink, and then dumps out the spaghetti. Jorie grabs his arm and takes a picture of the two of them on her phone. "I'm setting this as my background!"

Eli looks at the picture.

"Well," I say. "I think things are under control now."

Eli is supposed to say, "Don't go."

Nope. He stands there.

I storm over to the pot of sauce and furiously turn off the burner. "This is done!"

That kiss? I was right. Just a moment. What was I thinking? He likes her. They've probably kissed a hundred times. I'm just the cook.

Jorie scoots herself up onto a counter, crosses her legs. "Hey, we should make brownies!"

Thomas points his sword in her direction.

"You could really hurt someone with that," Jorie says.

He growls.

Thomas, I want to say, *I couldn't agree more.*

I stomp home, mad at myself. I just let her take over. She stole number fifty-one. He rang *my* doorbell. But what was I supposed to do, wrestle Jorie for the spoon? Take a cuter picture on my phone?

Eli didn't exactly seem to be stopping her. Right. Because they're going to HC. The whole neighborhood knows.

Fine.

I'm so done with this.

38

The next day, Sariah and I go to a clinic for girls who are thinking of trying out for the freshman basketball team. Her mom drops us at school. Sariah's mom looks just like Sariah, and she tells us to have fun. No warnings. What a concept.

Sariah and I stand at the entrance to the gym, watching the girls warm up. "They're gigantic," Sariah says.

One girl sinks a three-pointer. "And amazing," I say.

"We'll be benchwarmers for sure. If we even make the team."

A coach sees us. "You here for the clinic?"

"Um, yeah," I say.

"Well, grab a ball."

We start shooting around with the other girls. I'm out of practice, missing a lot, but it doesn't matter. It feels so good just to move, sweat, clear my head. Love the sound of twenty basketballs bouncing on a gym floor.

We do some drills, then a scrimmage game. Sariah and I barely get the ball. The three-point girl is also a ball hog. The coach pulls her aside after the clinic.

"I bet he wants her to come to the varsity tryouts," Sariah whispers.

"Maybe we should consider something else," I say, and smile. "The debate team? Student council? Fencing?"

"You're not serious? Have you ever fenced?"

"No! I wasn't serious. I wouldn't trust myself to handle one of those long swords."

Sariah laughs. "What about the art club? They make all the posters and flyers for school events. I really want to join. Come with me to the first meeting? Please? No tryouts."

Why does Jorie pop into my head? She'd say the club is full of weird kids; no one there would be a potential homecoming date. Maybe they are weird. Am I?

"Okay, I'll come." I smile. "Fifty-two."

"Great! What's fifty-two?"

"Oh, a good number."

—⟶

That night, my head is too full and I can't fall asleep. Everything's tumbling around, like clothes in a dryer. Mom, Grandma, Matt . . . Sariah and the art club kids . . . but mostly Jorie and Eli on homecoming night. Her red dress and his matching tie. Him kissing her.

I finally get up and put on a pair of flip-flops (shoes, for once), then slip out the back door into the dark. It's after midnight.

A perfect night. Black, cloudless sky. Warm, steamy air. I settle in the hammock, tuck my hands behind my head, close my eyes, and listen to the quiet.

Only, it's not quiet. Muffled voices. Laughter. A light in the Dixon house. And for the first time, movement. A blur of a face. Has Mrs. Millman been right all along? The Dixon house *is* haunted?

I roll off the hammock. Someone, or *something,* is definitely in there.

I cross the street. Should I call the police? Wake my parents? Where is Mrs. Millman when you really need her?

I stop on the sidewalk. The weeds are swaying

188

by the front window. If I see something (ghost or person), I will tear back to my house and get my parents.

Then I hear this laugh.

I freeze.

No.

I inch my way through the dark. Peek through the glass door by the patio in the back. Matt is sitting on the floor of the kitchen, with three other guys, in a circle. Two flashlights point toward the ceiling, lighting the room in an eerie way. They're all wearing dark sunglasses and caps, looking at something in between them. What? There are a bunch of bottles and chip bags around them, like the garbage I found.

This is where Matt's been going all summer? *Here?* I stand on my tiptoes, but I can't see what they're doing.

He broke in?

Like what happened at school. When he got suspended.

I sink into the moist grass. Is he drinking too?

I thought he was doing so well. He'd gotten it all together, with the job at the pool, getting into a decent college. Oh, Matt.

I'd never seen Mom and Dad get so mad. Mom yelled at him. . . . "This is serious. It's on your permanent record. A disciplinary suspension. This will affect everything. College. Your future. What possessed you?"

Matt said nothing. Stood there.

"Don't you have anything to say for yourself? Why, Matthew, why?"

It was a year ago, last May, when Grandma was dying. Matt and another kid broke into the principal's office, stole the elevator key, and went joyriding for an hour before someone caught them. They wrote graffiti on the elevator walls too.

"You made a bad choice, and now you have to live with the consequences. Don't screw up again."

Matt had detention and loss of school privileges and had to spend two Saturdays cleaning the elevators. Mom and Dad had to pay for a new lock too, and Matt had to pay them back. That's when he shut them out. Me too.

Matt turns his head and sees me. He lowers his sunglasses and we lock eyes.

Maybe Eli's right. . . . Is everyone too messed up for good things to matter? Can doing good really do any good? Make a difference?

Someone shouts, "Show me the money!" and Matt looks back and laughs.

All I want to do is run. From Matt, Eli and Jorie, my

parents . . . from this whole in-between, I-don't-know-what-I-was-trying-to-do-anymore summer of good things.

I even want to run from myself. For dreaming up the whole idea.

39

I take off.

The door slides open. "Nina!"

It's Matt, but I don't stop.

I run, like that day with Eli, except it's just me. No one to hold my hand.

I sprint to our patio and throw the cushions off the love seat, then turn and tear out of the neighborhood. I make it only as far as the park before I get dizzy and my legs feel like they're going to collapse. I plunk down onto a swing and start pumping my legs. More and faster and more and crying. Until I'm swinging high in the night, above the treetops, legs out and tucked in, again and again, drawing the thick summer air into my lungs. So high that I'm leaving the seat with every upswing. Gripping the chains tightly. Like this is the only thing left to do that makes sense. Swing. And breathe.

When I run out of energy, I let the swing slow. And stop.

I look at Grandma's wedding band on my finger. Why isn't she here to help me? No one else is that patient, or calm, or honest. I can't remember all the Simple Truths by myself. Why didn't she write them down for me?

I know she didn't want to keep going. . . . It was too hard. She never wavered. But that decision also meant she would leave me.

One of the last things she told me was "Love your mom. She's the kind of person who needs love more than she can give."

Even when I was little, I had this feeling of trying to reach out for Mom. Like her love was there but just beyond my grasp. She held on to her love tightly, like she didn't want to let it go. I thought if I was funny, or looked really pretty, or did good in school, she'd love me more. The way I wanted her to.

I used to think Grandma didn't get how hard Mom can be to love sometimes. But now I know that's why she told me. She knew she wouldn't be here anymore to love Mom, so I had to take over.

And Matt. He's a lot like Mom. Holds things in. He's been hard to love too.

The swing next to me moves slightly. I turn my head and see the fox across the park. Just like before, she looks right at me. She has one tail.

And I remember something else I read that night when I looked up the meaning of the *kumiho*.

In some legends, a fox possesses wisdom, courage, and the ability to step back and see its surroundings from a unique perspective. Because of its ability to camouflage and become invisible, a fox is an animal of in-between times and places.

A faithful guardian. Like me.

She is so beautiful.

The fox is still for a few more breaths, and so am I.

Then she's gone in the night.

And one of Grandma's STs comes to me: When you make up your mind to do something and you know it's right, don't let anyone tell you different.

40

It's the thought of Thomas that really saves me, though.

Running through the park with his cape, fighting the bad guys he sees everywhere. Believing in super-heroes. Believing that I am one.

I walk slowly out of the park.

All these things I've been doing.

They're like stitches. Some are neat. Others you have to tear out and redo. But in the end, they're connected.

I turn the corner and see the circle of eight houses.

A different perspective from the way I drew it for art. Where's the vanishing point?

The Dixon house is dark. Matt and his friends must have left. I look at my own house.

This whole time, this entire summer, I've been doing things for the neighbors, but what was I really trying to sew back together? Or who?

41

Matt is avoiding me, and Mrs. Millman is out to catch a ghost. If I tell her there isn't one, she will ask how I know. I've sent Matt a few texts, but he hasn't responded. I think he slept at a friend's after I saw him at the Dixons'.

At nine o'clock the next night, the Millmans, with Beanie at their side, set up watch. Mrs. Millman is dressed in all black, wearing a headlamp, and she has a camera strung around her neck. Mr. Millman is loading a backpack with a first-aid kit, a flashlight, and water bottles, and the staticky cell phones are on his lap.

They are sitting on chairs on the sidewalk in front of the Dixon house.

"Just what do you expect to accomplish tonight, Myrna?" Mr. Millman asks.

She holds up a small white plastic box that's beeping every few minutes. "This is an EMF detector, Stan. Electromagnetic field. Very sophisticated. If there are ghosts in there, this will locate and track them. We take a picture, and get proof."

"Then what?"

"We will ask the spirits to stop haunting the people in this neighborhood and move on."

Mr. Millman crosses his legs and shifts in his chair. "So we're going to sit here all night until a ghost appears on your little detector, kindly ask if it would mind posing for a photo, and then demand that it fly away."

"In short, yes."

"Myrna, we have been married for forty-two years. I've lived through your suspecting that your brother wasn't really your brother, believing my boss was on the terrorist watch list, and thinking my cousin was in the witness protection program. But this, this takes the cake."

She shakes her head. "There are things going on in that house. I have been saying it all summer, but no one believes me."

Mr. Millman sighs. "I'll say one thing. You do know how to keep life interesting."

She smiles and takes his hand.

They grow quiet. The sky darkens. And they wait.

I'm about to go inside. Nothing's going to happen. I'm sure what she saw was the shadows of Matt and his friends. The Millmans spent all this money on ghost tracking equipment when, as Dad said, there must be a perfectly reasonable explanation—

The EMF detector starts beeping wildly.

Mrs. Millman jumps up from her chair and switches on her headlamp. "The ghost!"

Oh, God, please don't tell me Matt has been dumb enough to go back into that house.

Mr. Millman grabs the cell phones and hands one to Mrs. Millman, and the two of them tiptoe around the back, looking like something out of a Scooby-Doo cartoon. I'm right on their heels. They're standing in the weeds, staring into the kitchen, clutching each other. The glass door is open a crack.

"Look at that!" Mrs. Millman screams. "Take a picture! Take a picture!"

Mr. Millman grabs the camera from around her

neck and starts snapping like crazy. The flash is going off everywhere, and Mrs. Millman's headlamp is beaming like a lighthouse.

I peek around them. There's water on the kitchen floor, with a mist above it, circling in the stale air of the house. Then—a huge bang. Followed by rattling.

Mrs. Millman turns and runs faster than I've ever seen her move before.

Mr. Millman spots me. "I'll be damned," he yells, running after her. "For once in her life, Myrna is right."

I'm still at the sliding door. I pull it open. "Hello?"

Nothing.

"Hello?"

Maybe ghosts don't respond to "hello." Maybe I need Mrs. Millman's advanced equipment in order to make contact.

I take a step inside. I don't actually believe in ghosts. It has crossed my mind, like it has for most people, but I can't really buy into the idea. Which is too bad, because if I did, I could try communicating with Grandma.

"Matt? Is anyone here?" I feel like he's hiding upstairs with his friends, but the house seems to be empty. The mist has stopped swirling above the water on the floor. I walk around a little. There are some flies buzzing. It smells sort of mildewy. The water's all over but looks deeper by the sink. I hear a gurgling noise.

Wait. The sink?

Mrs. Millman's ghost could quite possibly be a leaky water pipe.

I slosh through the water to the sink and open the cabinet underneath it. Water is dripping from the pipe. Not only that, but there are full bottles and un-opened chip bags inside the cabinet. Matt's secret stash? What are those guys *doing* in here?

I pick up a bottle with a wet paper label, fearing the worst. But I'm relieved to see it's just root beer.

Root beer . . .

Right after Grandma died, Matt set up a game of war, opened two bottles of root beer, and asked me to play. I looked at him, feeling so raw and empty, and said, "How could you think of playing cards right now? That's so wrong."

He swiped his hand across the table, threw the cards onto the floor. I knew he was crying. He ran upstairs, slammed his door.

I should have run after him. Why didn't I? I should

have played. It's my fault too, how he closed up. I could have tried more.

I stare at the pipe, thinking, *If my parents find out . . . If someone reports this . . . If the Millmans come back . . .*

If Matt gets in trouble again, Mom and Dad said the college could withdraw his acceptance.

I kneel and try to tighten the part of the pipe where the water is coming from. Disaster. Water starts pouring out faster. I try to turn it the other way, but it doesn't move, and now my hands are wet and slippery.

This is a good thing that I can't do alone. Or anonymously. There's only one person I can go to. Eli. Even if I sort of hate him right now. I know he can help. He's been fixing stuff in their house since his dad left.

I sprint across the street and knock softly. *Please be here.* I knock again, a little louder.

No answer. I'm going to have to figure this out. I run into my house and grab a stack of towels and any tool I can dig out of the kitchen drawer. I barely know what they are, let alone how to use them. I'm running down the driveway with everything, when I crash right into Eli. The towels fall and a screwdriver clatters to the ground.

"Come on!" I gather them up.

"What's going on?"

"I'll explain when we get there."

"Where?"

"The Dixons'."

"What?" Eli follows me across the street. "Nina! Wait!"

Mr. Dembrowski is backing out of his driveway. He turns onto the street just as we reach the sidewalk in front of the Dixon house. When I look back, he's stopped. His window is open.

This couldn't be crazier.

"What's the trouble?" he asks.

43

"Mr. D.," I say, like I talk to him all the time. "Do you know anything about fixing a leaky water pipe?"

"As a matter of fact, I do," he says, pulling over and getting out. He's the most normal-looking person I've ever seen, in a pair of khaki pants and navy shirt. Not a criminal or hoarder. And of course he knows about fixing pipes.

I lead Eli and Mr. Dembrowski to the back of the house. "Oh, man!" Eli shouts. "What did you do?"

"I didn't do this!" I yell. "You think I did this? It

just happened! I'm trying to fix it! This is number fifty-three!"

They give me confused looks.

"The pipe under the sink is shooting out water."

Mr. D. says he'll be right back. I hand Eli some towels, then start throwing my stack onto the floor, trying to soak up the water. He's just standing there. "Are you going to help me?"

He unfolds a towel, puts it down, and starts moving it around with his foot. "You're going to need something more than towels. I'll get a mop, and the squeegee from my garage."

I nearly slip on a wet towel. "Good thinking."

Eli leaves as Mr. D. walks in with a metal box of tools. He goes to the sink, takes out what might be a wrench, and then lies on his back, half in the cabinet. In a few minutes, the water stops. He pokes his head out. His shirt is soaked.

"Oh, God, I'm really sorry," I say.

He stands. "It's all right. I'll stop home and change."

"Were you going to work?"

"I was."

"Is the pipe fixed?"

"For now. I'm not a plumber. I did what I could."

"Wh-what do you do?" I ask. "I mean, your job?"

"I'm a security guard."

I nod. "Oh." Makes perfect sense. I gesture to the room. "Really, I didn't—"

"I figured."

Eli walks back in with the mop and squeegee as Mr. D. packs up his tools and glances at his watch. "I haven't been late to work in five years. The last time was when some neighborhood kids ran through my flower bed."

I bite my lip, but he picks up his toolbox and smiles at me. "It's good to be late once in a while. Life doesn't get boring that way."

He squishes across the towels, nods at me, and goes out the door. I think Mr. D. and I are okay.

"That was weird." Eli looks around the kitchen. "Should I even ask?"

"Not unless you want to hear a ghost story."

"Huh?"

"It's complicated," I say, and sigh.

Eli shoves aside some of the wet towels and starts using the squeegee to push water in the direction of the glass door.

It occurs to me that number fifty-three is different. And remarkable. It was a good thing with two other people.

As I kneel and try to sop up the water, I can't help it, I look at Eli's back. His shoulders, his arms. These curly parts of his hair over his ears. *Stop! Stop looking at something you can't have.*

I pick up a towel and go outside to wring it out on the patio. When I come back in, Eli grabs the mop and shoots water at me.

"Hey!"

He does it again.

I throw the towel at him.

Mop, squeegee, towels, water. We're soaked, and I'm not sure the floor is any drier.

He comes close. Touches my chin. We're inches apart.

"What about Jorie?" I whisper.

He shakes his head. He's about to kiss me again.

And my parents choose this moment to arrive on the scene.

Dad's voice calls from the doorway. "Nina? What's going on in here?"

This is not good.

"Nina?" Mom says slowly, her brows creased. "Why are you in here?"

Dad eyes the towels, the water, the open cabinet. "What happened? Did you do this?"

"No. I was cleaning it up."

He walks across the towels on the floor and peers under the sink. Eli and I take a step away from each other.

"Dad—"

"Mr. Ross," Eli says. "Nina came to get me, and—"

"What a mess," Mom is saying, looking around. "I can't believe this. We're going to have to contact the realtor. I'm not paying for this."

My head starts hurting. "Mom! Why would you have to pay? I didn't do it!"

Dad picks up one of the bottles, examines it. I see his face. He knows. "This isn't your fault," he says, "is it?"

I remember Mom saying to Matt, "You made a bad choice. Don't screw up again."

"It wasn't Matt!" I shout. "It was a bunch of teenagers! I don't know who they are! They were in here."

"You saw them?" Mom asks.

"Y-yes!"

Mom and Dad look at each other. Dad's shoulders sink a little. He shakes his head.

"I swear!"

My fingers are crossed behind my back. I turn around and look at Eli. Is this a good thing? I'm lying. My head is pounding so much, it's hard to think straight.

Dad takes hold of my arm. "You're coming home, right now. Mom and I will deal with this water situation later. Nina, this is breaking and entering. Vandalism. You need to tell us everything. Do you understand?"

"I didn't break in! The door was open!"

I can't even look at Eli. Like I'm five, Dad pulls me out of the Dixon house and keeps a tight grip on my arm.

A few minutes later, we sit in chairs at the kitchen table.

Mom has been unusually quiet, but then she says, "Just tell us, Nina. It was Matt, wasn't it?"

"The root beer," Dad says. "He drinks it all the time."

"No," I say, keeping my voice steady. "That's a co-incidence. I heard some noises, went over there, and a bunch of kids ran out of the house. The pipe was leaking, and the floor was flooded when I got there."

Mom and Dad aren't convinced.

Mom says, "Why was Eli there?"

"He was helping me clean up."

"Why didn't you come get us?"

"You? Aren't you *preoccupied*? The *case*? You'd have said, 'In a sec, honey,' and then never come. Every night, you sit here and work. That's all you care about anymore."

Mom looks shocked.

"You have absolutely no idea the pressure we are under," Dad says.

"You are the one who has no idea!" I cry. "About anything."

"Nina, that's not true." Dad's voice cracks.

"Let's stick to this situation." Mom folds her hands. "You're absolutely positive you don't know the kids?"

I stand. All I can think about is the way I felt when Eli was close to me. Wanting to kiss him so much.

Dad rubs his forehead. "If you withhold information, in a way, you're just as guilty. We're trying to keep you out of trouble. It's for your own good."

My own good. Right.

"Was it Eli?" Mom says. "I wouldn't be surprised. His father is a deadbeat. Everyone knows that. You don't need to be hanging around with him or getting involved in his problems. Pretty soon they become your problems."

I glare at her. "This isn't *Romeo and Juliet*. Eli's one of the best people I know. He's nothing at all like his dad."

"Don't be too sure."

"Grandma was right! You make it so hard!" I scream. "Can't you just, for once, not be so harsh about everything?"

Mom stares at me. "Don't change the subject, Nina. We're not talking about Grandma now. Or . . . me."

Dad glances at her, then reaches for my hand. "Nina, honey, if someone saw you there, if you know something—"

I pull away. "I don't expect you to get it, but I was trying to do something good."

45

Fine and Ross send me a text the next morning that their case is down to the wire and they won't be home until very late. *Try to stay away from other people's problems today,* Mom writes. Is she being funny?

I go back to the scene of the crime. The glass door is shut. I peer inside. Eli must have finished cleaning everything up. The towels, mop, and squeegee are gone, and the floor looks dry.

The Millman house is strangely quiet.

As I'm walking home, Jorie calls from her window. "Nina! I need you! Come up here!"

She has two dresses spread out on her bed—red satiny and purple flouncy. "Did you get my text?"

"No."

She groans.

Maybe these missed texts are a symbol of our friendship—hanging on by a few intermittent words.

She points to the dresses. "Which one?"

"For homecoming?"

"Duh."

I sit on her chair, the fuzzy one that makes my legs itch. I feel like the fabric is going to swallow me up. "Tell me the truth," I say. "Right now. Are you going to homecoming with Eli? Did he ask you?"

She picks up a bottle of nail polish and shakes it. "All I want to know is which dress you like better. I bought them both because I wasn't sure. My mom thinks—"

"Jorie."

"We're going." She pushes the dresses aside and flops onto her bed. "I'm just waiting for him to say yes. And he will."

"What do you mean?"

"Here's the thing, Neen. I got tired of waiting for him, so I asked. I mean, it was a done deal anyway, so what's the difference who asked who?"

I stand and scratch my leg. How does she sit on this chair? "There's a big difference. So you put the sign on his garage?"

"Yeah."

"He didn't ask you?"

"Right. So?"

"You said . . . All this time, you made it seem like . . ."

"We're still going. And I'm still trying to get Leo to ask you."

"And I told you not to do that. I don't want to go with Leo. Or Grady, or any other boy you think I should go with. I've been talking about going with Sariah and some other girls."

She starts playing with her hair. "Wait, Sariah?"

"She was at your party."

"Oh. You're friends with her?" Jorie rolls onto her side. "Why would you want to go with just girls?"

"We thought it would be fun."

She jumps up and squeezes me in a hug. "But I really want you to go with me! It would be way more fun with dates. This is high school! You know, the whole thing. Dresses, killer shoes, corsages, pictures."

"Why couldn't we still get dresses and take pictures? And wear killer shoes?"

"You could, of course, but it's not really the same."

I don't answer, and she looks at me. "What's the matter?" she asks. "You look sad."

"Jorie, you just say things, and you don't even think about how someone might feel. How I feel."

"I'm sorry."

I walk to her doorway. "You push too hard sometimes."

She sits on the fuzzy chair, pulls her knees up. "I go
after what I want. Like I told you at my party, you
have to make it happen. My dad tells me that all the
time. What's wrong with that?"

I shake my head. "I need to go."

"Wait, you didn't tell me which dress you like
better."

"Wear both. Change halfway through the dance."

Jorie gasps. "I never thought of that! Should I do
that? I could do that!" She frowns. "But how would I
get the other dress to the dance? I could ask my mom
to bring it."

I've given her something to think about for the rest
of the day. This is too sad to count.

I am going to finish the sixty-five good things if it kills me.

54. I go around to the back of Mr. D.'s and water the forget-me-nots. Several more green sprouts have appeared. Grandma is popping up everywhere.

55. I put a note in his mailbox that says: *Thanks for your help the other night. I hope you weren't too late for work :) From, Nina Ross.*

56. I send my brother a serious text: *Stop avoiding me. We need to talk.* I hope it goes through.

Nine more to go.

47

Eli is at my door with the towels, folded and stacked. Dry and extremely clean.

"Although I suck at making pasta, I've gotten pretty good at laundry," he says, and smiles. "You have any laundry questions? I'm your guy."

I take the towels. "Thanks. For washing them. And cleaning up. I would have helped, but . . ."

"No problem."

We stand there, awkward.

I so badly want to ask him what's going on

with homecoming, but then I'd be like Jorie. Pushing.

"Was it really some kids who broke in?" Eli asks.

I don't answer.

"It's okay. You don't have to tell me."

Over his shoulder, I see Mrs. Chung. Riding a bicycle. Actually, a tricycle.

I put down the towels and step outside. "Look, Mrs. Chung got her cast off." I point. She's riding in slow circles around the cul-de-sac on this sort of adult tricycle with a metal basket in the back. Her leg looks normal again. She waves to me, and I wave back.

Eli shakes his head. "You are . . ."

"What?"

"I don't even know how to describe it. You're like so hopeful all the time." He looks at my feet. "And you have some sort of anti-shoe thing going on."

I smile. "What can I say?"

Behind Eli's back, Mrs. Chung gives me a thumbs-up.

Eli walks onto the grass and pretends he's shooting a basketball. "Well, I should go."

Something happens. I'm suddenly seized with this urge to just . . . I've never done anything like this before. I run up, jump toward his face, and kiss him on the lips.

Mrs. Chung stops her tricycle and softly claps.

He leans down and kisses me back. Right there. On the warm grass. Under the bright sun.

Except.

I see a flash of hair from Jorie's window.

She saw. She knows. Oh, God. I'm dead.

48

What have I done? My life, and the Fertile Crescent, are a mess.

Two days later, Jorie won't talk to me, Eli has disappeared again—maybe something to do with his dad—and Matt hasn't texted me back. My parents seem to have forgotten about the Dixon break-in and are working more than ever. And the Millmans haven't left their house in days.

I hear Mrs. Cantaloni telling Mrs. Chung that Mrs. Millman is now suffering from post-traumatic stress syndrome. The same thing Beanie has.

"I've been bringing over groceries. Poor Stan is worried sick about her. She's on medication. Apparently, they really did see a ghost in there," Mrs. Cantaloni says.

Mrs. Chung narrows her eyes.

"That place could be haunted." Mrs. Cantaloni rubs her stomach. "I mean, don't you think there's lots of things in this universe we know nothing about?"

Mrs. Chung nods slowly.

The Cantaloni boys are tumbling across their lawn. "Do not push your brother, Jack!" Mrs. C. shouts. "How many times have I told you that?" She marches toward them. "Jack! Jeremy! Jordan! Inside, now!"

The boys bolt into their house, Mrs. Cantaloni follows, and Mrs. Chung pedals off on her tricycle. Thomas crashes through the bushes and trots toward me.

"What's up?" I ask.

He scratches a mosquito bite on his arm. "The girl over there?" He points toward Jorie's. "She came over to my house and yelled at Eli." His eyes get big. "She's mad at you," he whispers. "Real mad."

I sigh.

"But Eli was mad at her too. They were yelling so much, I had to cover up my ears!"

My heart flutters. "Why was Eli mad?"

Thomas puts his hands on his hips. "About the sign she put on our garage. I'd be mad too if somebody hanged a sign on my house and I didn't want them to."

A white truck pulls into the cul-de-sac.

"What's that say?" he asks.

I read the letters on the side. " 'IPIT. Illinois Paranormal Investigative Team. For all your ghostly needs.' "

"I can't believe this," I say as Thomas holds up his sword.

This guy in a navy jumpsuit gets out and knocks on the Millmans' door. It opens, and he disappears inside. A few minutes later, he comes back out with the Millmans. Mrs. Millman has circles under her eyes. She's wearing a gray sweat suit, and her hair's sticking up.

They start walking around the Dixon house. The jumpsuit guy is holding a little tape recorder and talking into it. Mrs. Millman must be recounting the ghost sighting.

"This is completely crazy," I say to Thomas. He runs over to the sidewalk and points his sword at the Dixon house. "Pow!"

Mr. and Mrs. Millman and the guy stand and talk a little more; then finally the guy gets into his truck and drives away.

Mr. Millman pats Mrs. Millman softly on her back. "They'll take care of it, Myrna," he says. "Don't you worry. We'll get rid of that ghost."

Thomas runs back to me. "This is the most exciting place in the world!"

Fifty-seven?

49

Jorie is pounding on my door.

"I am not talking to you," she says as she storms in. "I just came over to tell you one thing. You're wasting your time. Forget about it."

Jorie has looked better. Hair in a messy ponytail. No lip gloss. Old cutoff shorts. Puffy, red eyes.

"What are you talking about?"

"Him." She tips her head in the direction of Eli's house. "He's asking someone else. Not you. Not me."

Swallow. "How do you know?"

"He told me."

Take a breath. "Who's he asking?"

"I don't know. It's killing me. He wouldn't give me a name. He just said, 'There's this other girl.' I stalked him on Facebook, but I couldn't figure it out."

I sink into the sofa. I get it now. I get the whole thing. Eli comes off as this really sweet guy, taking care of Thomas and asking for help with pasta, but he's a player. All summer, he's been flirting with both of us, and he was planning on asking another girl. Probably someone gorgeous, in honors classes and a star athlete and on student council, amazing in a million ways.

Jorie crosses her arms. "I saw him at school with Tyler's cousin. It's probably her. We've both been completely stupid."

She takes a tissue from her pocket and wipes her nose. "Why did you kiss him? You knew I liked him. We're *friends*. You don't do that."

She's right. "I'm sorry, Jorie, I really am. I didn't mean for it to happen. I swear."

"How can you not mean for it to happen when *you* were the one who kissed him?"

I look down. "He kissed me first. Last week."

"What?" Her face crumples. "How did that *happen*?"

"He was upset, his dad came over, they were fighting—"

Jorie drops onto the floor, then starts to cry. She

225

covers her face. Her shoulders are shaking. I fall next to her, crying too. We're sitting cross-legged, our knees touching. But she moves away. Her mascara is running black rivers down her cheeks.

I choke back a sob. "You're a mess."

She sniffles. "Yeah, because of you."

I get her another tissue and she dabs her eyes, then looks at me. "I can't just forgive you. I wish I could go back to being little. It was so much easier."

I put my arm around her. "I know."

She shakes off my arm. "I'm still mad. I never thought you'd do something like this. Other girls, yes. Not you."

"I'm sorry, Jorie. I really am. I didn't flirt with Eli. He and I are friends. I was just trying to help him."

She gulps. "I thought I knew you."

I look at her teary blue eyes. She stands, straightens her shoulders, pulls down her shirt. Then slips out the door.

Things happen when they're meant to happen. Did I mean to hurt Jorie? I wanted to kiss Eli. . . .

Grandma didn't explain that there could be complications.

50

It takes this.

A change of heart. Sticking to my story. And a heat advisory.

When I wake up the next morning, Fine and Ross are home. Sitting in the kitchen in their bathrobes. Strangely quiet. An empty table. Mom staring out the window.

"What's wrong?" I ask them. "You're scaring me."

Mom looks at me blankly, then picks up her coffee cup. "Did I finish this?"

"An hour ago." Dad makes her a fresh cup.

"I knew this could happen—of course it's always a possibility—but in a million years, I never thought it would," Mom says.

Dad scratches his unshaven chin. "You never know what's in people's minds."

"What happened?" I ask.

"Melanie," Mom says, "had a change of heart. She called us early this morning with big news. After all their arguing, hating each other . . . this whole legal mess . . . she decided to go back to her husband."

"Really?"

"It happens. Hearts are a funny thing," Dad says.

Mom smirks. "Hearts? He bought her a five-carat diamond ring. She said that made her realize just how much she still loves him. So. We're done. She dropped the case."

"Wow," I say. "Just like that?"

Dad nods. "Just like that."

"I give them six months," Mom says, sighing.

Matt sort of drifts into the room. "What's going on?"

For the first time in a long time, the four of us are in the same room at the same time.

"Did someone, like, die or something?" Matt says.

"Their client dropped the case," I answer.

Matt raises his eyebrows, leans against a counter, avoids my eyes.

"Apparently it's on the news," Dad says. "We haven't watched."

Mom gets up and stands at the patio door. "You know there's a heat advisory today? For the next few days too. My mother used to say the heat makes people crazy."

"Simple Truth?" I ask.

Mom looks at me, nods slowly.

"You're taking this much too hard, Erica," Dad says. "We should go downtown. Get on with things."

Mom shakes her head. "Not today. I got so caught up in it. All those billable hours . . . It doesn't feel as good as I thought it would. I'm irritated and . . . just really tired."

The four of us stand there. Cold air is coming from the vent by my feet. The sun makes a prism on the table. The coffee machine is blinking—add water.

Dad looks at Matt. "We haven't had a free minute until today, but we need to know, Matthew, were you in that house across the street the other night? Tell us the truth."

"I told you," I say, before Matt can answer. "I saw some kids running away. Why don't you believe me?"

"You always jump to conclusions—" Matt says.

"If you've done something again—" Dad says, clenching his jaw.

"It wasn't him!" I shout. Fifty-eight. I think.

Long silence.

I have to do something. Now. Fast.

"Let's make breakfast," I blurt. "I'm starving."

The air conditioner clicks off. A few seconds go by.

"Now that you mention it . . . ," Dad says.

Matt shrugs. "I can always eat."

Mom digs in a cabinet, takes out a frying pan. "I think I still know how to scramble an egg."

"You're *really* scaring me now," I say.

She laughs. Wow.

Dad sits down, sips his coffee. "Erica, you know something? I was all right with the old Fine and Ross. Before Melanie turned us upside down. I think we need some perspective."

Mom's cracking eggs. Her shoulders drop a little, but she doesn't answer. And then I notice there's something in her wardrobe that isn't black. Her bathrobe. It's pink with little flowers, and it belonged to Grandma.

"Perspective is good." I start opening cabinets. "Ms. Quinlan says that's the basis of everything."

"What are you looking for?" Mom asks, measuring pancake batter.

"Those glasses."

"Which glasses?"

"I found them." The fancy ones, from the lemonade a long time ago. They're dusty.

Miraculously, we have strawberries. Matt wipes the glasses while I rinse the strawberries and cut a slice in four of them. Matt and I set the table. Fifty-nine. Wow again.

Scrambled eggs. Burnt pancakes. Slightly expired orange juice, which Dad says is still drinkable. Strawberries on the rims. The four of us at the kitchen table. Small talk. A joke. Dad cutting the pancakes like he used to cut spaghetti.

Not perfect. A little rusty.

But still a family.

After breakfast, Matt's sitting in my hammock.

I sink onto the grass next to him.

There's so much to say, but we're silent. I don't know where to start.

Finally he says, "You didn't tell them you saw me in the house."

"Right."

"But then, I don't get it. Why do they think I was in there?"

"They saw the root beer on the night of the flood."

"What flood?"

"A pipe burst. The kitchen floor flooded. The Millmans thought it was a ghost. Mr. Dembrowski, Eli,
and I were cleaning it up when Mom and Dad found
us. They were positive it was your fault."

Matt is staring at me "A ghost? Mr. Dembrowski?
What?"

"Long story."

"Well, you didn't have to cover for me."

"But I did."

"Why?"

"Dad said if you screwed up again . . . they could
take away your college acceptance. Your whole future
would be messed up."

He gets up. The hammock swings wildly. "Look, I
just needed somewhere to go, okay? To get away from
everything. Everyone. Don't you feel that way sometimes?"

"Yes, absolutely."

He jumps and pulls a leaf from the maple tree, then
tears it in half. "We just wanted a place to hang. We
didn't think anyone would find out. It wasn't like the
time before, at school—I swear, Nina. We didn't steal
anything."

"But you broke in."

Matt shakes his head. "The lock was already
broken."

"What were you guys doing, anyway?"

He shrugs, smiles. "Playing poker."

"Poker?"

"Yeah. Okay, so I have this goal. . . . I haven't told anyone. . . . I want to play in the World Series of Poker. I'm getting good. I play in online tournaments too."

I remember the day he taught me. "I beat you, though."

He laughs. "Beginner's luck."

"Oh, okay, that's what you call it?"

He swipes at a tree branch. "I'm sure Mom and Dad will be thrilled. *Great goal, Matthew. Get serious. Have you considered law school?*"

"I still don't get why you went to the Dixons'. Why couldn't you just play at one of your houses?"

"Not the same. It was private. We could stay up as late as we wanted, be loud."

I nod, remembering the night I saw them with their sunglasses and caps. They were just playing poker. That's all it was.

Matt sighs. "Okay, maybe it wasn't such a brilliant idea. We haven't gone back. I guess I owe you. But you owe me too."

"What are you talking about?"

He smiles. "I saw you that day. Planting Mrs. Chung's flowers."

My heart skips a beat. "You did?"

"I was in my room. Then when I was leaving, she came up to me, asked if I'd seen anyone. She was shaking, Nina. She couldn't understand it."

"What'd you say?"

He narrows his eyes. "I told her, 'Don't worry. Some things in the universe, you just have to accept without question.' "

That sounded a lot like one of Grandma's STs.

"Matt?"

"Yeah?"

"I'm sorry I didn't play cards with you that day after Grandma died."

He nods. "It's okay."

A car pulls up. Two guys are inside. "Ross," one calls. "Let's go, man."

Matt looks at me. "I'll tell Mom and Dad the truth. I swear."

His friend beeps the horn.

I pull out a chunk of grass and throw it at him. "Go play some poker."

"Okay, Nina green-a."

I have reached number sixty.

Remarkable.

52

The IPIT truck is back.

It's dusk, that in-between time when night and day cross paths. The leaves on the trees are wilting, the air is thick. It's the third day of the heat advisory.

The Millmans are in front of the Dixon house, talking to three guys in navy jumpsuits. Mrs. Millman looks more normal. For her.

"This is much too big for Stan and me," I hear Mrs. M. tell them.

"If there is a ghost here, we will find it," one of the

jumpsuit guys says. Their jumpsuits say IPIT on the back, along with GOT GHOSTS?

Some of the neighbors come outside. Mrs. Chung. Mrs. Cantaloni, who is enormous now. She's talking to Mrs. Bennett. Jack, Jeremy, Jordan. Thomas, with cape and sword. Jorie's parents. Mine.

"What's going on?" Dad asks Mrs. Millman.

"The other night," she says, "Stan and I encountered a ghost inside that house. These men are from the Illinois Paranormal Investigative Team. They're trained to take care of matters like this."

Dad stares at her. "You saw an actual ghost?"

Mrs. Millman nods vigorously, and Mr. Millman pipes in, "I saw it too."

"It's best if you people move away from the location," one jumpsuit guy says, motioning to us. The other two are positioning a tall ladder against the side of the house.

Everyone slowly walks into the middle of the street.

"Exactly what did you see?" Jorie's dad asks.

Mrs. Millman closes her eyes, as if the memory is too painful to recall. "Water. A swirling mist. Rattling, knocking. And a distinct sensation that *we were not alone.*"

Mrs. Chung nods. "Fox spirit."

Dad and Jorie's dad roll their eyes.

"I don't know what it was. A ghost, or a fox spirit, but something otherworldly is definitely occupying that house," Mrs. Millman says. "And we need to do something about it. Ask it to leave us alone. Once and for all."

"I'm sure there are other explanations," Dad says.

"Have you talked to the realtor about all this?" Jorie's dad asks.

Mrs. Millman puts her hands on her hips. "Oh, he's right there with me. We're good friends now. He believes in spirits, too. I have his permission to finish this investigation."

The jumpsuit guys are pulling out all this equipment: little metal boxes like the one Mrs. Millman had, a video camera, a couple of regular cameras with huge lenses, and flashlights. They put caps on their heads. They bend down and tighten their shoelaces.

"We're goin' in," one of them calls. "Don't touch the ladder. We might need to get onto the roof later." They head toward the back.

Dad glances at me, then Mrs. Millman. "Hold on a second. Water? And you say this was a few nights ago? You saw water inside the house?"

"Yes."

"In the back? In the kitchen?"

Mrs. Millman gasps. "You saw it too?"

Suddenly Matt is next to me. When did he get here?

Thomas circles around the group, thrashing his sword in the air. I can see the flashlights and the outlines of the jumpsuit guys through the windows of the Dixon house.

"Nina?" Mom says. "Was that the same night?"

Mr. Millman points at me. "You saw it, didn't you? You were right behind us!"

Everyone looks at me. "Yes, but . . . I don't think it was a ghost. Really, Mrs. Millman. It was some kids. And Mr. Dembrowski fixed the leak—"

"Mr. Dembrowski?" She shakes her head. "No, I'm positive! The ghost turned on the water. I've heard they can do things like that."

Matt walks toward Mom and Dad. Mrs. Chung is explaining the legend of the *kumiho* to Jorie's mom, who looks confused.

"Uh, Mom, Dad," Matt says. "Can I talk to you?"

One of the jumpsuit guys comes running toward us. "We're getting a reading!" He sprints back around the side of the house.

Thomas runs across the street, his cape streaming behind him, sword held high. He reaches the bottom of the ladder propped up against the house. "I'll get the bad guys!"

"Thomas! No!" I call, but he's already up a few rungs.

I run toward the ladder. He's high up when he drops

the sword. It falls silently, doesn't make a sound when it hits the ground. Thomas looks behind him. "My sword!"

And then the streetlight goes out. And the lights in the houses. The entire neighborhood is dark.

53

I grab the bottom of the ladder. "Thomas! Don't let go!"

"Nina! My sword!"

"Don't worry about the sword. Just hold on!"

I start climbing. The ladder shakes. It's hard to see Thomas clearly.

I hear Dad yell, "Those ghost guys must have blown a circuit!"

Jorie's dad: "I'll call Com Ed!"

"Nina!" Thomas's voice is trembling.

"I'm coming! Stay there!"

Mom and Mrs. Cantaloni are at the bottom of the

ladder, looking up. Mom steadies the ladder. "Nina, be careful!"

My hands are sweaty. Legs wobbly.

Finally I wrap my arms around him. He's safe. We're safe.

His bottom lip is trembling. "I was going to get the bad guys."

"Thomas. You've been getting them all summer." Me too.

He smiles.

I let out a breath. "Let's go down together, okay?"

Rung by rung, little by little, me holding him, him holding me. Eli and Mrs. Bennett are watching us.

Mrs. Bennett grabs Thomas in a tight hug. "Don't ever do something like that again."

"What were you thinking, Tom?" Eli kneels next to him.

I find the sword in the grass and hand it to Thomas. I'm shaking. Sixty-one.

Mom puts her arm around my shoulders.

Thomas looks at me. One superhero to another. It's not an easy job.

The paranormal guys are still walking around the Dixon house with flashlights, and I see their shadows. Or the ghosts. Who knows anymore?

Mrs. Cantaloni clutches Mrs. Bennett. "Oh my God. My water broke."

54

Mom rushes to Mrs. Cantaloni's side, and she and Mrs. Bennett help her walk. "We'll drive you to the hospital," Mom says.

"I don't know if there's time." Mrs. Cantaloni grimaces, taking a couple of steps. "This baby's coming fast."

"Let's get you inside," Mrs. Bennett says calmly. And to Mom, "Call the paramedics." Mom's peering at her phone, punching in numbers. Dad runs over with a flashlight and shines it on Mom's phone.

"Jim's on his way from the city," Mrs. Cantaloni

says. "I've had contractions all day, but they were far apart. I thought I'd make it."

"This'll be interesting in the dark," Mrs. Bennett says. "We need more flashlights, everyone."

Mr. Millman rushes over with the headlamp on. "I'll be your labor coach!" He takes Mrs. Cantaloni's arm. "Now breathe!" They all help Mrs. Cantaloni into the house.

"Oh, Stan." Mrs. Millman puts a hand over her heart. "Fathers weren't allowed in the delivery room when we had our boy," she says to the rest of us.

I didn't even know they had a son.

"He lives in Boston," she tells Mrs. Chung, who's holding a huge flashlight. "We're going to visit him in the fall."

The Cantaloni boys are skipping across their lawn. "We're having a baby!" Jordan shouts.

"It better be a boy!" Jack says. "Girls are yucky!"

"I like girls!" Jeremy says, and his brothers tackle him. Thomas jumps in too.

Jorie comes out with a pink flashlight. Her mom has pulled two chairs to the end of their driveway. She sits on one and pats the seat of the other. Jorie sits next to her. I notice that her mom has lit the aromatherapy candle I put in their mailbox weeks ago. It gives a soft glow to both of their faces. Her mom turns the chair and says something. Jorie is listening.

Eli comes up next to me.

"I need to ask you something," he says.

My heart jumps.

"What's this ring you've been wearing? Did Grady Brunson give it to you?"

"What?"

"Are you going to homecoming with him?"

"Grady?"

"Jorie kind of hinted that you were."

"Me and Grady? No."

"You're not going to homecoming with him."

"No!"

"Really?"

"I swear. I've barely ever talked to the guy. He thinks my name is Gina."

Eli smiles and picks up my hand. "So who gave you the ring?"

"It was my grandma's wedding band."

He nods.

An ambulance, fire truck, and police car pull up. Sirens blaring. A Com Ed truck is right behind them. Two paramedics leap out of the ambulance and run into the Cantalonis'.

"Nina. I do remember that night we ruined Mr. D.'s flowers. But what I remember most is hiding in back of Mrs. Chung's. With you."

"I remember it too."

"So."

"So."

"Don't go anywhere." He runs into his house and comes back with a pen.

"Are you going to take notes?" I say.

"Shut up." He smiles and takes my hand again, the one with Grandma's ring. And he writes: *HC?*

The other girl?

It was me.

It was always me.

55

Eli and I sit on the curb at the circle of grass in the middle of the cul-de-sac. Thomas skips in front of us, laughing. "Eli and Nina, sittin' in a tree, *K-I-S-S-I-N-G!*"

"Well," Eli says, grinning, "if Thomas says so."

He kisses me, and I kiss him back.

Eli nods. "You've convinced me."

"About?"

"That there are more good people in the world than bad."

I take his hand. "I knew you had it in you."

Sixty-two. Almost there.

Jorie shines the flashlight in our direction. Her mom gently lowers Jorie's hand.

I look down. "All this time, I thought you were going to homecoming with Jorie."

He looks uncomfortable. "I liked her in the beginning of the summer, but then it wasn't working. It wasn't right. I didn't know what to do. She's so . . ."

"Hard to say no to."

He laughs. "Yeah."

Mom comes out of the Cantalonis'. She walks toward Matt and Dad, standing by our garage. Their voices are low, so I can't hear exactly what they're saying, but from the looks on Mom's and Dad's faces, Matt is telling them what happened at the Dixon house.

Dad doesn't seem to be freaking out, and Mom isn't lecturing. They're just talking and listening.

This is a such good thing. Sixty-three. I'm not even doing them anymore; other people are. They're just happening.

That little flame inside my heart has jumped out and is making its way around the sidewalk, lighting the circle of houses.

56

Jorie leaps from her chair and walks over. Eli jumps up, goes over to Thomas, and starts tossing a ball with him and the Cantaloni boys just as their dad drives up and rushes into the house.

Did she tell Eli that I was going with Grady so Eli would go with her? If so, then she did something bad too. But I guess it doesn't matter anymore.

I bite my lip. "Hi."

"This is crazy." She waves her hand.

"I know."

She scratches her cheek. "My mom said I should come and talk to you."

"You're here because your mom said?"

"Yeah." She sinks down next to me. "No. This is all such a mess, I don't even know where to start. I liked him so much, and you really hurt me . . . but I think I always knew . . . he liked you."

I nod. "Thanks for saying that."

"Anyway." She shakes her hair. "Guess what?"

"What?"

"Grades asked me!" She holds up her phone, shows me a text: *Hey, wanna go?*

I laugh. Grady *would* ask in a text. "I thought he liked *you*," I say.

"I know! I don't know why I didn't see it before. So really, I need your advice. *Which dress?* Mom said I can't have both."

"Jorie. You are one of a kind."

"So are you, Neen."

"Red!" I shout.

She hugs her knees. "Okay!"

I call to Eli. "Help me with something?"

"Another flood?" he shouts.

"No. C'mon." I get up. "Jorie, you too."

She hesitates but then follows me and Eli to my patio. I put the cushion on the love seat, and the three of us carry it to the end of my driveway. Then we go back for the chairs.

Jorie is doing that corner-of-her-lip smile. "You're so weird, Nina."

"I know. This guy from my art class, Chase, told me to 'Stay weird.'"

Jorie and I lift a chair. Our eyes meet as we set it down beside the love seat. She breaks the connection first, pushes her hair off her forehead, steps back.

A police officer is sitting in his car. I think he's the one who came that day Mrs. Millman called, suspicious over the Hershey's Kiss and penny in her mailbox.

"Looks like you're having a party," he says.

Mrs. Chung is bringing over a chair. "Why not?"

Jorie's mom drags her chairs to our driveway. Then Mrs. Millman carries one over too. She has Beanie on a leash. Mom, Dad, and Matt are there. Mom sits on the love seat, looks my way, and pats the cushion next to her. A place for me.

Jorie curls on the ground by her parents. Eli pulls Thomas onto his lap.

The candle is flickering by Jorie's house. A dozen flashlights. A million stars. It's amazing.

"This is something," Mom says.

Mrs. Bennett and Mr. Millman are still inside with Mr. and Mrs. C. and the paramedics. Flashlights shine from their windows. The Cantaloni boys are running bases on their lawn.

I've almost forgotten about the IPIT guys until they come out and start loading equipment into their truck. One walks over. "Well," he says. "It's gone."

Mrs. Millman's mouth is hanging open. "What was it? What did you see? An orb? A poltergeist?"

"We're not exactly sure, but I can assure you the spirit has left that house."

Everyone looks stunned.

Except Mrs. Millman. She's ecstatic. She picks up Beanie and cuddles her. "You're safe again, darling."

"You saw a ghost?" Dad says.

"Yep. See 'em all the time," the guy says.

"All the time?" Jorie's dad repeats.

The guy nods. "Oh, they're out there. You have to believe."

Matt grins at me. "Some things you just have to accept."

I grin back. "Right."

"Anyway, we'll send you a bill," the guy says to Mrs. Millman. "Sorry about the power outage. Where's your husband, by the way?"

She waves toward the Cantalonis'. "He's in labor and delivery."

"What a crazy neighborhood," the guy says.

"It must be the heat," Mom says, and smiles at me.

57

"I knew it!" Mrs. Millman says as the IPIT truck pulls away. "I have a sixth sense. People have always told me that."

Beanie barks, as if she agrees.

Jorie's dad is shaking his head. He looks like he's going to say something, but Mrs. Chung starts singing in Korean. Beautiful words in a high, clear voice. Everyone's quiet. Even Beanie.

Then she sings two lines in English: "Just as there are many stars in the clear sky . . . there are also many dreams in our heart."

She stops. "I used to sing this to my children. And my father sang it to me."

"That was lovely," Jorie's mom says.

"I can sing too!" Thomas says.

Everyone laughs, and Mrs. Millman sighs happily. "The neighborhood is back to normal at last."

Mr. Millman dashes outside. "It's a girl!" he shouts.

"Oh my God." Mrs. Millman jumps from her chair. "Heaven help her, with three older brothers!"

"What's her name?" Jorie's mom asks.

Mr. Millman is beaming. "Julia. Julia Rose Cantaloni. They think she's eight pounds, maybe more!"

"Big baby!" Mrs. Chung says.

"You were eight pounds, two ounces," Mom says to me.

"I was?"

"Uh-huh."

Then Julia Rose and I have something in common. I like her already.

"You have a baby sister," Jorie's mom calls to the Cantaloni boys, who have continued to play this whole time. "How do you like that?"

"She better learn how to play baseball," Jack says.

"She could pitch," Jeremy suggests.

"I'm the pitcher," Jordan says, and stamps his foot.

"Let her learn to walk first," Mrs. Millman says.

"And baby and Mom are both doing fine," Mr. Millman reports. He turns to the house. "They're taking them to the hospital. Come quick!"

Mrs. C. is being wheeled out on a stretcher, Mr. C. walking by her side. Mrs. Bennett is carrying the baby in a blanket. Everyone else walks over. Julia has a head full of dark hair, like her brothers, and her eyes are squeezed shut. She's the smallest person I've ever seen. The boys fall over each other, running to see their new sister.

Mrs. Bennett hands the baby to one of the paramedics.

"Guys," Mrs. Cantaloni says to her boys. "You're staying the night at Thomas's house. Dad will see you in the morning, okay? I hear Thomas has a few extra swords."

They jump and scream, "Hooray!"

Mrs. Chung is standing next to me. "Nothing in the world like a new baby," she whispers. "Makes everything possible again."

The neighbors drift back to their chairs as the ambulance, fire truck, police car, and Mr. Cantaloni pull away. The Com Ed truck is still here, working on getting the power restored. I kind of like it this way, though. Quiet, dark, the cul-de-sac lit only by the glow from flashlights.

Mom's eyes are red. "I remember when you and

Matt were born like it was yesterday." She sniffles. "Oh, what's the matter with me?"

Dad hands her a tissue. "I told my brother we're taking him up on his offer to use their cabin. A vacation! No arguments."

Mom nods. "Okay."

She and I sit back down on the love seat.

She pulls something from her pocket. "I found it."

"What?"

"The recipe."

"The carrot ring? Really? Where was it?"

"Scribbled on the back of another recipe." She hands it to me, and I look it over.

"I'll never be able to make it like she did."

Mom puts her arm around me and gives me a little squeeze. I don't know if that qualifies as an actual hug, but I'll take it.

"Maybe not," she says, "but you'll make it your way."

If that's not a Simple Truth, I don't know what is.

Mom can be hard to love. But that doesn't mean I don't.

I'm sure that's how Grandma felt too.

"I love you," I say.

She sniffles and smiles and sighs and says, "I love you too, Nina."

Sixty-four.

58

I am wearing shoes. Beautiful strappy, silvery shoes with the highest heel I've ever worn. So high, I'm not sure I can walk that well.

And the blue dress, which was miraculously still in the store when Mom took me to the mall. So it was meant for me.

Sariah was there buying a dress too. A really pretty dark green. She said, "Frog green." We cracked up, but the salesgirl didn't think it was funny. Sariah's going with a group of girls and we'll be at the same after-party. I can't wait to see how she looks.

Jorie took my advice. She looks amazing in the red dress. Like she's about twenty. Hair piled up in curls, French manicure and pedicure, spray tan.

Mom has told me a hundred times that I look beautiful, but I kind of knew that.

Almost everyone is outside. Same eight houses. Brown, white, tan. But nothing is the same.

Mrs. Chung has turned on her Christmas lights so her trees sparkle in the September sunset. Tonight, the neighborhood looks like something out of a fairy tale. If it wasn't already.

The air is cool, and summer is almost gone. Mrs. Cantaloni holds Julia in a blanket, and I'm glad to see that Mrs. C.'s stomach is returning to normal. The Millmans are there, with a healthy-looking Beanie by their side. Mr. D. sent me a note that he was sorry to miss everything, but he put a couple of the delicate, sky-blue forget-me-nots in a pot and left it on our doorstep. So a part of Grandma is right outside my door.

And Eli. In a suit and light blue tie. Wow.

He grins and says, "Nice shoes, Neen."

I laugh and take his hand.

"Nice everything," he says.

Mrs. Chung brings each of us a marigold. "It's a flower of love," she says.

Mrs. Bennett and Mom make us pose for a hundred

258

pictures; Mom is texting some to Matt. He left a few weeks ago, promising me he won't break into anything at college. And he said he'd miss me and I'd better visit. He said we'll play poker but he won't let me win so fast.

Grady and Jorie are taking pictures in her driveway. He's wearing red Converse shoes with his suit. They look cute together. They fit.

I suddenly think, *Sixty-five! I forgot to do the sixty-fifth good thing.*

But then I look around, and realize sixty-five is right in front of me. It's everything.

I hold out my arms and spin around, our circle of houses blurring, my dress floating. Grandma's wedding band is snug and secure on my finger. There isn't a vanishing point in a circle. At least that I can see.

Mr. Millman points to the Dixons'. "Someone bought the house!" A sticker on the For Sale sign says SOLD!

"Oh, boy," Mrs. Millman says. "We'll keep an eye on that place, won't we, Beanie?"

Beanie barks. Mrs. Chung nods and says, "Me too. I'll bring lunch."

Everyone laughs.

Without a doubt, this is number sixty-five.

Thomas is at my side. He got a buzz cut for kindergarten and he looks so much older that I catch my breath. But I'm happy to see the sword tucked into his shorts.

"Mystery Girl!" he shouts. "You look so pretty!"

I lean down. "Shhh! You're not supposed to tell anyone."

"Aw. Everyone knows."

Eli and I get into the back of his mom's car, and I put the marigolds on the seat between us.

Because that's how everything started.

"Ready?" he asks.

I am.

Appendix

The Sixty-Five Good Things
by Nina Ross

1. Freaked out Mrs. Chung by planting her marigolds.
2. Cleaned up and organized about a hundred toys in the Cantalonis' yard.
3. Put a Hershey's Kiss in the Millmans' mailbox.
4. Left a rose on Mr. Dembrowski's doorstep.
5. Placed a good luck penny in every neighbor's mailbox. Or a magic coin, depending on your perspective.
6. Watered Mrs. Chung's marigolds.
7. Brought mail to her door.

8. Untangled plastic bag from her tree.
9. Hung up her wind chimes.
10. Baked brownies for Mr. Dembrowski.
11. Gave foot pads to Mrs. Bennett.
12. Left aromatherapy candle for Jorie's hyper dad.
13. Gave Mr. Millman cigars, despite risk of tongue cancer.
14. Picked up Jorie's lip gloss on the bus.
15. Delivered treats to Mr. D.
16. Delivered more treats to Mr. D.
17. Made chocolate chip cookies for Matt.
18. Found Cantaloni boys' baseball in the weeds.
19. Cleaned out Matt's car.
20. Brought Matt's old baseballs to the Cantalonis.
21. Stuck smiley face "Have a nice day!" balloon into the Millmans' flowerpot.
22. Made Eli laugh (hit his arm with a crab apple).
23. Gave the color wheel to Amber.
24. Complimented Jorie.
25. Watched Thomas.
26. Took Thomas to the park.
27. Comforted Thomas when his cape tore.
28. Discovered that a pillowcase can be used as a substitute cape in emergencies.
29. Sewed Thomas's cape.
30. Told Sariah her drawings were amazing.
31. Drafted Thomas into the Cantaloni baseball league.

32. Bought a bone for stressed-out Beanie.
33. Wrapped up two slices of Mrs. Bennett's banana bread for Mr. Dembrowski.
34. Gave a bottle of lotion to Jack Cantaloni for his mom. Exploded on his shoes. Fail.

(Hid from Sariah in store. Go back ten spaces. . . .)

35. Complimented Jorie's mom.
36. Played left field during Camp Nina.
37. Left a pot of marigolds on Mrs. Bennett's front step.
38. Put a *You're welcome* note in Mr. D.'s mailbox.
39. Put Matt's smelly shirt in the laundry.
40. Planted forget-me-nots in Mr. D.'s yard.
41. Watered forget-me-nots.
42. Watered all the marigolds. Neighborhood in bloom. Consider career in floral industry.
43. Brought golf balls over for Mr. Millman.
44. Fixed Thomas's cape again.
45. Cleaned up garbage in back of the Dixon house.
46. Told Jorie's mom I'd watch out for Jorie.
47. Mrs. Millman held a neighborhood meeting because of what I've been doing. More poeple outside at one time than I ever remember.
48. Said hi to Sariah at Jorie's party.
49. Talked with Mom.
50. Marathon run with Eli (first kiss!).
51. Helped Eli cook spaghetti. (Side note: Jorie stole this one.)

52. Agreed to join art club with Sariah.
53. Fixed leaky pipe with Eli and Mr. Dembrowski.
54. Watered forget-me-nots.
55. Left thank-you note for Mr. D.
56. Tried to get Matt to talk to me.
57. Thomas said our neighborhood is the most exciting place in the world.
58. Didn't tell on Matt.
59. Matt and I set table for family breakfast.
60. Told Matt to go play poker with his friends. He called me Nina green-a!
61. Got Thomas down from the ladder. Superhero bonding.
62. Eli came over to the good side.
63. Matt, Mom, and Dad talked.
64. Told Mom I love her. She said it too.
65. Homecoming.

If I did it, anyone can.

Acknowledgments

I started this story with a question: does doing good really do any good? Random acts of kindness are everywhere, but I wondered, do they really have an effect on people? Can small acts of goodness change our world? I also worried that the dizzying variety of electronic communication available at our fingertips was actually making families and neighborhoods more disconnected than connected. Out of these thoughts grew *The Summer I Saved the World*.

My enormous gratitude to Wendy Lamb, who urged me to go deeper and brought out the best in me and this story. In the early versions, I think she knew more about the story than I did! To Dana Carey, for her many reads and spot-on advice, and to Samantha Rodan for sharing her enormously helpful comments. To Heather Daugherty for her amazingly gorgeous cover design and Bara MacNeill for her meticulous copy editing. And to Alyssa Eisner Henkin, agent extraordinaire, who loved this book from the very start and saw its potential. I would happily do sixty-five good things (and more) for all of you!

To my favorite librarians (and friends), who have been there for me in so many ways: Sherri Bolen and Susie Pasini; I am indebted to both of you. And to my wonderful circle of family and friends: you inspire me in more ways than you realize.

Finally, to my husband, Ben, and my children, Rachel, Sam, and Cassie, who support me every day by listening, counseling, keeping me grounded, and always reminding me what's most important.

To all of you, thank you from the bottom of my heart.

The answer to my question—does doing good really do any good—I will always hope, is a resounding and undeniable yes!